IF I FALL

IF I FALL

IF I FALL

a novel by
ALEX BLADES

If I Fall: A Novel by Alex Blades

This edition published in 2024.

Copyright © Cody A. Blades 2019

Printed in the United States of America

SECOND EDITION, PAPERBACK

ISBN: 978-1-7357839-3-2

Fiction: Contemporary Romance
Fiction: Romantic Comedy
Fiction: LGBT/Gay

For all the hopeless romantics

chapter **one**

A deafening hiss roared from under the sink.

I ripped open the cabinet doors and drowned in a gushing stream of water, letting out a small yelp in between gurgling and gasping for air. I grabbed the roll of paper towels from the counter above my head and tried to clog the spewing pipe.

"Hello?" I screamed. "Adrienne? Help!" I continued stuffing paper towels around the pipe, only to be met with shreds falling apart in my hands. I hopped off the floor and started turning the handles again. Nothing. The hissing from beneath the sink continued and drowned out my shrieks. "Hello?" I yanked open the kitchen drawer, pulled out the pile of dish towels, and held them against the hole in the pipe to prevent the small pond already forming in the floor from getting any larger.

"Son of a—"

The gushing slowed to a stop and I melted into the floor, staring at the heaping pile of mushy paper towels and the stream of water rolling across the warped floorboards. The water dripped from my clothes as I stood and I knew I picked a bad day to wear mesh shoes. There's nothing worse than wet socks.

"You're cleaning all that up, just so you know," I heard from behind me.

I whipped around, nearly slipping and falling on my face. "Adrienne! You can't just sneak up on someone like that!" I twisted the bottom of my shirt and more water hit the floor. "Where were you? I've been yelling your name."

She played with the curly ends of her dark brown hair. "Well, while you were screaming like a little girl, I was finding the main water shut off."

"I—uh . . . I was gonna do that next."

"Mhm." She picked through the front closet and pulled out a large white towel and the mop leaning against the wall. She stepped over the settled puddles and handed them to me. I dabbed at my sopping wet hair and face.

Adrienne Santiago was one of my best friends from college. She was one of the first few people I talked to when I moved into the dorms, besides my roommate, whom I hadn't spoken to since we roomed together. There were very few people that I still talked to from college after we made the move to New York. That's just how it goes, I guess. As you get older, you realize that you were only friends with some people because you were with them all the time.

"Thanks," I said. The stream of water rushing across the kitchen slowly vanished as I ran the mop along the trail.

"Someone needs to call Derek so he can get out here and get it fixed."

"Already texted him," Adrienne said. "Of course, he said he wouldn't be able to get out here until the end of next week, but when I threatened to sue, he magically changed his mind. He'll be here in a couple of hours."

I finished wiping up the water and trekked into the living room, throwing the mop back into the broom closet along the way. My sopping wet clothes dripped onto the black and white striped rug and my waterlogged shoes squished against the floor as I made my way down the hall to my bedroom. "I thought you were supposed to be meeting your teacher friends from work."

"I thought about it, but then I realized I didn't really want to. If anyone asks, I've been running a fever all day."

I threw on a pair of dark blue skinny jeans and a grey and white button up I'd managed to score at half price and walked back out into the hall. "Great, that means you can wait for Dipweed to fix the plumbing again while I go out and grab some dinner for the dragon lady." I sprinted to the bathroom and ran some more product through my hair, trying to create the effect of having some sort of wave to it. I was cursed with my mother's straight, plain brown hair.

"Ooh, I wish I could, but I really don't want to. Plus, I have to go out and run some errands," Adrienne said, staring at me from the doorway. "Hey, on a scale of one to like . . . killing me . . . how annoyed would you be if you came home to a redecorated living room? Hypothetically speaking, of course."

I glanced at her through the mirror in between trying to put in my contacts. "Well, hypothetically speaking, I thought we'd agreed to wait until we can actually afford to do a bunch at once and we could pick stuff out together."

"What if—hypothetically speaking—we had more than we thought saved up and I know what you like."

"Well then don't spend too much and keep your receipts. Hypothetically speaking, of course." I did another quick check of my hair in the mirror by the front door.

"Pick me up something yummy."

I changed into my dark brown chukka boots, threw on my favorite jacket, and yanked my keys off the hook by the door and ran off down the stairs and into the bustling city streets.

Even after spending the last ten months of my life in the Big Apple, I still wasn't quite used to the wafting stench of exhaust leaks and cat urine. I pushed my way through the ocean of people, occasionally receiving a glare or two from someone I bumped into.

I would be lying if I said I immediately grew accustomed to the hustle of the city and all of its residents. People can definitely be—for lack of a better word—rude. Even though I still hadn't fully adapted to everything that went on in the city, it's still safe to say I fell in love quickly. There was never a dull moment.

It really was the city that never sleeps.

It was also insanely beautiful and half the time I felt like most of the buildings were too fancy for me to get into wearing just a t-shirt and a pair of jeans. We didn't have anything like that back home. Their idea of fancy was Friday night dinner at the Olive Garden twenty minutes away.

I passed the stairs leading down to the subway and instantaneously got the shivers. There was no way in hell I was going down there, no matter how much someone offered to pay me. It was just so creepy to think about being trapped underground with a bunch of smelly weirdos like I was a rat or something, so that was out of the question. They say a real New Yorker walks everywhere, so that's exactly what I intended to do after I figured out how expensive a city cab was.

I stopped at the edge of the sidewalk across the street from a little restaurant with a big sign on the front that read *Mateo's*.

Time for a little bit of honesty: I wasn't there to pick up lunch for the dragon lady. I was there to have lunch. With a living, breathing person. On an actual date. I hadn't been on one since the move when I figured out most New Yorkers are kind of assholes.

I felt super terrible about lying to Adrienne about it, but her being aware of any sort of dating life on my part was bad news. She would want to know every little detail, like how we met and what our first date was like, and I just didn't have time to deal with all of that.

I did one last quick check of my hair in the reflection of a nearby car and straightened out the collar of my shirt. I steadied myself and caught my breath before pushing myself across the road and inside. I scanned the perimeter of the restaurant and the many patrons. I clenched my fist and nibbled on the inside of my cheek as I strolled along.

"Hello, welcome to Mateo's. Is it just one?"

"Actually, I'm meeting someone here. The table should be under Danvers."

He scrolled through the tablet in front of him. "Right this way, sir."

The man led me through a maze of tables and chairs toward the back corner of the building. I could feel my heart pounding mercilessly against my chest the closer I got. I glanced down at my feet, unable to fully take in what was happening.

Dating was always something that made my anxiety max out. I could feel the panic building up and I had to fight the urge to turn the other way and run out of the building. In all honesty, I may have run off if my date hadn't looked up and seen me.

The host motioned me to my seat, and I sat down across from my date. I tried not to stare at his hypnotizing blue eyes or extremely full lips.

"Your server today will be Amanda. Can I start you guys off with some drinks?"

"Just a water please," we said in unison.

"Great, I'll get that right out for you."

I took a moment to catch my breath again while I fiddled with the rolled-up silverware on the table. I finally looked up and we locked eyes. It all hit me. I was really doing it.

I bit into my lower lip, instantly tasting a subtle hint of blood on my tongue. Someone scraped their fork across their plate and I snapped back to reality, shaking my head. I let a sigh slip from my throat.

"You okay over there?"

"Huh? Oh . . . right . . . sorry. I probably look like a total weirdo right now," I said.

Really, Noah? That's what you decide to lead with?

"Not that I'm weird or anything. Or maybe I am just a little bit. I don't know. I guess I'll have to let other people be the judge of that." I fanned myself with the drink menu. "Is it really hot in here?"

I was really making a great first impression.

"Hey, it's cool. Just be yourself," he said. "Want to just start over?"

"That would be great."

He extended his hand toward me. "Hi, I'm Bennett Danvers."

"I'm Noah Carlisle. It's great to meet you, Bennett."

We spent the next couple of minutes looking over the menu, most of which was him telling me what was worth ordering. I wasn't sure if that meant he had been on several dates there in the past or if he just enjoyed the restaurant. Either way I was avoiding the less than desirable choices I usually made with food. Last thing I needed was to have the unwavering stench of garlic on my breath or spinach stuck in my teeth.

After I finally picked through and found what I wanted, we spent the next minute or so discussing our top five favorite musicals. I'm not exactly sure how we even managed to get on the topic, but it was amusing, nonetheless.

"Hi, guys, sorry for the wait. My name is Amanda and I'll be taking care of ya'll today," our waitress said, pulling a notepad and pen out from her apron. "Are ya'll ready to order or do you need a little more time?"

"I think we're ready," Bennett said. "Can I get the tomato basil chicken and instead of the brown rice can I substitute grilled asparagus?"

"Of course. And for you?"

"Um, I'll actually have the same."

"Alright, I'll get your orders back to the kitchen. Is there anything else I can get ya'll?"

"I believe we're all good," Bennett replied. "Thank you."

"Great, just let me know if ya'll need anything. I'll take these menus and get out of your hair."

We handed her our menus and I slowly lifted my water glass. I could feel the moisture in my mouth evaporating away, as if I'd just finished gorging on an entire pack of saltines.

I set down my glass, wiped my damp palms on the legs of my pants. My heart was pounding again and I was convinced it would explode at any moment if I wasn't careful. I folded my hands along the edge of the table and took in a deep breath, allowing it to fully expand my lungs. As I fidgeted around in my chair, I heard a loud thumb from under the table and a twinge of pain zipped through my leg, radiating at my knee.

"That sounded painful. Are you okay?" he asked.

"Yeah, I think so," I lied. I took another deep breath. "So, what is it you said you did again?"

"Well right now I'm working at Phoenix Public Relations. I'm hopefully up for another promotion."

"That's really great."

"And what about you?" he asked.

"I actually just got a job about nine or ten months ago at Hale Publishing working as an assistant. I'm just starting out, but it's exciting work so far."

His eyes lit up and he shot a smile in my direction. "That does sound exciting. Did you always want to go into that type of work?"

"Sort of," I replied. "Stories have always been my number one love. While I would prefer to be the one *writing* the books, this is still extremely rewarding itself."

"Well, maybe one day you'll be one of those few lucky people getting published by Hale."

"Maybe."

I felt his leg brush against mine, sending a shock up my spine.

The two of us spent the next forty-five minutes discussing anything from what we would bring to a deserted island (a book about how to build a small boat out of trees and the tools to do it, obviously) to what television shows should never get a revival in the age of remakes, all in between eating the food I for once didn't regret ordering.

"So, what was it like actually growing up in this city?" I asked.

"It was interesting. Sometimes it can be a bit much, but you never find yourself bored."

"How *could* you get bored here? It's the exact opposite of where I was raised."

"Where did you say you're from again?"

"A tiny town in Illinois called Lakeview. It's kind of a hole in the wall and if you wanted something fun to do you would go to Walmart with your friends at four in the afternoon. It closed down like a year ago though, so I'm not sure what they do now."

He took another sip from his glass as I checked the notification on my phone.

"You have to leave already?"

"No, it's just my roommate showing me some new stuff she bought for the apartment. She loves redecorating."

"Sounds a lot like my friends," he laughed. "How long have you guys known each other?"

"Freshman year of college. It's been awesome living here together, minus a few hiccups."

"That happens. Does she have any idea where her ridiculously sexy roommate is right now?"

"You're too kind." I blushed and hid my face behind my hands. "But she doesn't know where I am. I know it's probably the last thing you want to hear, but I've kind of dealt with quite a few bumps along the road with guys. I just want to take things one day at a time and wait before I say anything to anyone." I ran my fingers along the tablecloth. That was the moment that I had been dreading all day.

"Hey, that's okay."

"Really? Because the last time I told a guy that I wanted to take things slow he ran out on me mid-way through our date and I never heard from him again."

"Where exactly have you been meeting all these guys? And exactly how do I fit into all of this?"

"Same place I met you," I said.

"Point taken."

Bennett laughed and his fingers caressed mine. I paused for a moment before looking up and seeing some of the judgmental eyes glaring in our direction. I pulled back my arm and rested it in my lap.

He moved his hand back to his side of the table. "We all do life at our own pace. I know I've dealt with a few bad apples, and it really sucks. I totally get it, and there's no pressure on my end."

"Are you sure you're real and not just a really great dream?" I asked.

"I promised myself I wouldn't be one of those douchebag guys. The world would be a much better place if everyone treated each other like human beings."

"Again, I have to be dreaming right now or you have to have some weird flaw that you're not telling me about. A tail maybe? Or a third nipple? Something."

He laughed again and I couldn't help but let an embarrassing grin slip through.

My phone vibrated against the tabletop again. It took everything I had to not chuck it across the room into the fish tank. If it wasn't for me being a poor boy and a new phone being way out of my price range, there was a fat chance I might've.

"I'm sorry, she doesn't normally—"

9-1-1! Get here quick, Adrienne wrote.

"Is something wrong?"

"Uh, I—I don't know. I'm sorry, but I really need to go. I'll text you later."

Running out in the middle of a first date wasn't exactly the smoothest move, so I wasn't holding my breath on ever hearing from him again.

Story of my life.

chapter **two**

I sprinted through the front doors of my apartment building and up the five flights to the unit. I could still feel the adrenaline coursing through my veins and my heart was pumping as I dug my keys out of my pocket. Panicking, I struggled to find the keyhole for the deadbolt. Finally, there was a click from the other side of the door and my keys were pulled from clammy hands as it flung open.

"You're here!" Adrienne said.

"What's the emergency?" I asked, still panting. "Was there a fire? Did someone die?" I pushed my way passed Adrienne and into the kitchen. Nothing seemed to be charred and everything seemed to be above water as it should be.

"So, I might have stretched the truth a little bit."

"What the hell? I was with—" I paused, " —my boss. What could possibly be so important that you made me think someone was dying?"

Adrienne grabbed me by the shoulders and twirled me around toward the living room. I regained my balance and focused my eyes on the blonde figure melting into the couch cushions.

"Zoe?"

Adrienne and I weren't the only ones to come to the city looking for a new adventure. Before the move, we were just some dumb college kids. We had the typical ride or die friend group comprised of people from our first year in the dorm, but it was different with Adrienne and Zoe.

I was used to being around a bunch of people, having grown up with an older sister who had a new best friend every week, and I had never been on my own before. That made finding a supportive, family-like dynamic important for me.

That is exactly what I found with Adrienne and Zoe. The three of us were totally inseparable. I honestly have no idea how I would've made it through all four years of undergrad without them. It was us against the world. Or at least it was until Zoe met the love of her life after starting her new job, and then moved out shortly after.

We hadn't really had a lot of time to hang out together as a group since then.

"Hey." I looked down and her eyes were swollen and puffy. Her makeup had run down her face. "What's wrong, Zo?"

"We broke up."

"What? How? When? Why?"

"I'd rather not talk about it."

"That's fine. We'll talk when you feel ready," Adrienne said.

"We'll kill him," I said. "I've watched enough psycho documentaries. We can make it look like an accident."

Zoe chuckled in between sobs. "You don't have to kill him. Can I please just stay here for a bit? At least until I can figure out what I'm going to do. I really don't want to have to run back home."

I sat down next to Zoe and put my arm around her. She rested her head on my shoulder and stared down at the floor.

"Of course! You can stay here for as long as you need to," I said.

"Totally," Adrienne said. "We're always here if you need to talk about any of it."

"Thanks, but I'm kind of all talked out. I don't even want to think about it right now."

I rummaged through a shelf full of old DVDs and pulled out a copy of *White Chicks*, our go-to for any bad situation, and set it on the table in front of Zoe. "Triple T KA?"

"Look, I really appreciate the effort, but I don't think the Wilson sisters will cut it this time. I just really need to get out for a little while I think."

"I don't know. I have work in the morning, and those kids are a lot to deal with even when I don't have a hangover," Adrienne said.

"Just this once? Pretty please . . ."

"Come on, you know that I can't ignore the puppy dog face." Adrienne paused, tried to look away. Finally, she let out a sigh and rolled her eyes. "Fine, but only if Noah agrees to go."

And all eyes were on me.

"Not cool, guys," I said.

I never really got the whole point of going out and partying with a bunch of sweaty strangers, drinking until all hours of the night. I'm more than capable of having fun with a night at home cuddled up on the couch with a good book.

"What do you say? Are you in?" Adrienne asked.

"I don't think so. I have a meeting tomorrow morning and my boss has been breathing down my neck. I swear he can smell weakness."

"Come on, party pooper!" Zoe said. "Just this once, and then you can go back and crawl into your little reading nook when you're all done."

"Guys, it sounds like a lot of fun, but you know I'm not a morning person as it is, and my boss has me so stressed out right now."

"You're stressed out? Even more reason to go out and have some fun before you go back in there tomorrow morning. Besides, I have to go babysit a bunch of whiny teenagers tomorrow and *I'm* still going."

"I don't know. I just wanted to turn in early tonight and do some more work before I pass out."

Zoe grabbed me by the shoulders and pulled me closer. "No more excuses. You're going out with us tonight and we're not taking no for an answer, mkay?"

"You're not going to stop until I say yes, are you?"

"That would be a no."

"I guess one drink couldn't hurt. But I'm inviting Theo and Kara."

Zoe laughed. "The more the merrier. Now I need you guys to help me pick out an outfit for tonight because I need to look hot."

It was after 10pm when our Lyft finally pulled up outside the bar that Zoe found. In the few short months that I'd been in the city, I had never once been inside a New York City nightclub.

The mixed scents of sweat, cheap cologne, and one-hundred proof vodka hit me like a ton of bricks and triggered a gag reflex. The layers of dried up alcohol covering the floor clung to the bottom of my chukkas like static and I had to peel them from the floor with every step.

I followed the girls to the bar. "Okay, I came, I saw, and now I can go back home and proudly—or not so proudly, depending on how you look at it—say that I indeed went out."

Adrienne, who was already extremely buzzed along with Zoe from a bottle of cherry vodka and some soda from back home, grabbed my arms. "Your little ass ain't goin' anywhere, hunty! You're going to stay and have some fun with me."

"Ugh, but—"

"No excuses, Noah. I'm with Adrienne on this one. You work way too hard to not have some fun for once. Stay, mingle, dance, chat with some cute guys, and live a little for once. You never give yourself that opportunity."

I spent the good first year and a half of my college career with my head buried in books while I grazed on basically any snack food I could find in the dining hall. It was a completely new world for me at the time, and I think I used it all as a coping mechanism. The one issue with that was it really kept me from being social for the remainder of my college career.

Sure, I had the best friends that a guy could ever ask for, but I don't have much to show for my time in college except for my degree and a few pictures from back when I was fat.

"Okay, so I guess you might possibly have a little bit of a point," I said. "Just one drink and then I'm going back to the apartment so I can try to get some actual sleep."

"Mm, how about three drinks," Zoe argued.

"Two."

"You drive a hard bargain, but okay. Just so you know I would have agreed to only one. You're such a pushover."

"And you're an awful human being."

"I know, it's kind of a gift." Zoe flagged down the bartender. "Aye, can we get three Captain and Cokes over here. Please and thank you!"

I turned and glared at her.

"What?"

"You know that my tolerance to that stuff is low. Two and I'll be on my ass."

"Yes, I'm aware of that. You only get two drinks and we have to make em count, right?"

The bartender handed us our drinks and Zoe slammed the money down on the sticky, yet somehow slimy, bar top.

"Drink up!"

I looked down at my cup and regretted giving her free reign to choose what we drank. I got a whiff and was immediately brought back to the last time I drank it, most of which is a complete blur.

All I remember was downing about two glasses the night of the party that all our other friends threw for us before our move. I remember drinking some of it and dancing a little bit. The rest of the night was a blank and I woke up the next day on a friend's living room floor wearing absolutely nothing. I hadn't had a drop of alcohol since.

"Man up and drink it!" Zoe yelled.

I braced myself for a potential vomit session, tilted my head back, and let a good portion flow down the hatch. I felt the warmth glide over my esophagus and hit my stomach like a rock. "Agh!"

"I didn't say to gulp it. That's your own fault," Zoe said. "But that's my boy!"

Zoe threw back what was left at the bottom of her cup before getting another one for the both of us and dragging me out to the dance floor kicking and screaming. My head spun as I felt my drink finally hitting my system. My heart raced inside my chest as we danced along to the DJ's mix consisting of Justin Bieber, Taylor Swift, Post Malone, Maroon 5, and who knows who else. By that point I was too out of it to even care. I wasn't kidding when I said I can't really handle my alcohol.

Adrienne joined us shortly after holding a few shots of fireball.

I could feel my drink soaking further into my system every time my glass touched my lips. I was ready for more and the chances of me stopping myself from getting it were getting much slimmer. I hadn't felt that much weight lifted off my shoulders since I'd moved away from home and I didn't want it to end, even if it meant possibly hating myself for it in the morning. As I finished my second drink, I felt all my fears and worries slowly melt away. I pushed my way through the crowd toward the bar.

"I guess it's water and then bed now, right?" Zoe asked.

"Hell no! I'm just going to grab another one of these, anyone want anything?"

"Sure," Zoe replied. She followed me across the floor to the bar and grabbed the bartender's attention. "Two of the tastiest drinks you can make, sir."

"You got it."

I swirled around in my chair and watched everyone jumping around like wild animals in the middle of the dance floor. Even Adrienne was still feeling herself. I tapped my foot along to the beat of the new mix the DJ was playing and watched the pattern of the strobe lights in awe.

Two drinks and I was a goner. I sank into the stool, dangerously close to slipping off, and just took in everything. I thought about my life and how I wasted my college years with my nose in a new book every day. I thought about how instead of going out and living my life I chose the safer route and just read about the lives of others.

"Here you go, bud. Enjoy," the bartender said as he handed me my drink. "That'll be ten dollars."

Zoe handed him two five-dollar bills from her pocket. I took one sip and let it glide down my throat, feeling the immediate burn.

I hopped off my bar stool with my drink in hand and started feeling the full effects of everything I had been ingesting. My body somehow felt light as air, yet completely bolted to the ground at the same time. My legs quivered as I walked. I wasn't five feet from the bar when I felt someone's body topple into me, throwing me completely off balance. I held onto the nearest chair for dear life.

Zoe chuckled. "Dude, you really are a lightweight. You just stay here and chill and I'm gonna go find Adrienne."

She disappeared in the crowd right before someone else knocked into me.

"Aye, watch it bud—oh, Theo! You guys made it! Where's Kara?"

I wasn't sure if it was the drinks seeping in my system, but for the first time I noticed how gorgeous Theo was. I mean, I always thought he was cute with his sparkling brown eyes, dark curls, and amazingly clear skin. That night he just had a certain glow about him.

"She had to run to the bathroom. Noah, are you feeling okay? You're looking a little flushed."

"I feel great, dude."

"Are you sure you're okay? You're not looking too good."

"I'm all good, I've only had like three drinks. I just haven't had a drink since we moved here, so it's been like . . . months."

He was right, though. I wasn't feeling too great, so I can only imagine how I looked. It's embarrassing how little it took to do it. It was just the only time I didn't feel the crushing anxiety to do everything perfectly.

"Maybe you should slow down a bit? You don't want to be sick at work tomorrow."

"I'll be alright. I'm not that drunk."

Kara appeared from between waves of people. "That bathroom was so gross." She looked me up and down and pushed a stray piece of her auburn locks out of her face. "Noah, how much have you had to drink?"

"Only a few, I'll be fine," I said, not even believing the words coming out of my own mouth.

"If you say so."

I tried finding my balance while Kara ordered a beer for herself and Theo. "What do you think the meeting's going to be about?" I asked her.

"Probably just a bunch of promo stuff for the new book. Nothing we haven't dealt with before."

I found a chair and leaned back into it as I scanned the crowd for Adrienne and Zoe. I soon spotted the top of Adrienne's head in the much taller crowd. She was still dancing away in her own little world in the middle of the dance floor. "Would ya'll excuse me for a minute," I said before sliding off my chair and hobbling out into the parade of people.

When I finally found Adrienne again, she was drunk off her ass and scrolling through Instagram stories, bobbing along to the music as she went.

"Hey there, boozy," I said.

"Noah, there you are," she giggled. "I have been looking for you forever. Everyone here is so tall!"

"Adrienne, have you seen Zo?"

She continued laughing at her phone.

"Adrienne, where is Zoe?"

"Hmm? I don't really know. One second she was here and then . . . poof! Gone like magic. You should dance with me now!"

"Just give me a sec. I need to find Zoe." I turned my back, surveying the bar hoppers drenched in sweat and liquor. I found several blondes, but none of them her.

I was beginning to realize just how bad of an idea the night was.

"Ope, I found her!" Adrienne said. "She's over there." She pointed to the corner next to the bathrooms. "Grinding with that guy."

I marched across the room, despite my body being ready to collapse at any minute and everything spinning all around me. The ever-so-subtle smell of vomit and tequila danced around my nostrils the closer I got to the bathrooms and I was ready to make my escape.

I reached out for her hand. "Zo, come on. We're going home now."

"Okay, bye."

"We didn't come here so you could dance with whatever prick decided to buy you a drink. We came so you could distract yourself."

"And this is getting my mind off—" Zoe paused for a moment, "—what was his name again?" she laughed and took another swig of her drink.

"I think we've had enough fun for one night. We all just need to go home and get some sleep," I said.

"Who died and made you my boss? I'll leave when I'm good and ready to leave. Right now I'm dancing with . . . uh . . . Jake? Tim? Whatever his name is. I'm having a good time and I'm not ready to leave yet."

I grabbed her by the arm, which was probably not the wisest decision.

"Get your hands off me! I'm not going anywhere yet. You wanna run home, then just go. I don't need a babysitter. I'm a big girl."

"Fine, you want to stay here? Then you can stay, but I'm not gonna stay here and be treated like roadkill."

I grabbed Adrienne and stormed outside. After that, it all kind of went blank. Or at least I think I grabbed Adrienne. I don't even remember getting home that night. The only thing I was certain of the next day was that I never wanted to go out drinking ever again.

chapter **three**

I was startled to life by several police sirens zipping down the street.

As I rolled off the couch onto the floor, I let out a small groan. I peeled my face from the cold wood and brushed my fingers through my hair. Light rays peeked through the sheer white curtains and I stared blankly into the muted television screen. I stumbled to my feet, my head still reeling from the night before, and staggered into the kitchen.

I grabbed a bottle of water from the fridge and practically inhaled it, trying to get rid of the funky taste still lingering in my mouth from whatever the hell the bartender sold me. I wasn't sure what was in it and I was in no rush to find out.

Looking down I realized that I was standing in nothing but a pair of underwear with no memory as to what happened to my clothes between getting home and waking up. I tossed my empty bottle into the garbage can and continued staggering through the apartment and into my bedroom.

I stepped through the doorway and was hit by the mixed odors of tequila and greasy food with a hint of vomit. I leapt over the pile of my clothes from the night before, which seemed to be the source of the stench, and grabbed a white t-shirt from my closet.

As I slipped it on over my head, I caught a glimpse of the clock on my nightstand and realized I had less than forty-five minutes to shower, get dressed, grab something to eat that wouldn't upset my system any more than it already was, and get to work without my boss ripping my head off.

This, ladies and gents, is precisely why I now have a rule against consuming alcohol on a Thursday night, even if #ThirstyThursday is trending on Twitter.

It wasn't until I'd finally made it to the corner of Fifty-seventh and Third that I had realized I never talked to Zoe or Adrienne about what happened at the bar. I wasn't even sure if they had made it home or not or why I was passed out on the futon instead of my own bed.

It was then that I also realized I had only five minutes left to make it to work.

A text from my boss yelling at me came through about the big meeting with our most prized author, Cordelia Collins, or as I liked to call her due to her demanding and terrifying personality, the dragon lady. Anything Cordelia wanted, she got, even if that meant me pulling all-nighters making sure every little detail of her new book release was perfect. The woman was completely ridiculous and a total diva. She was the queen of the literary world.

I lunged through the front doors of the office building, nearly toppling into a lady with half a dozen iced coffees in hand and sprinted for the elevator doors. Any time I stepped into those elevators I was painfully reminded as to just how claustrophobic I can be at times. Having about nine other people piled into a metal box with me hanging above the ground can have that effect on me.

I clung to the uncomfortably warm handrails of the elevator and I listened to the ding as we stopped at each floor. Floor four. Floor five. Floor six.

My anxiety rose and suddenly I was aware of the fact that I was sandwiched between a middle-aged woman reeking of vodka and cigarettes, the stench I became all too familiar with at the bar, and a guy who somehow smelled of various cheeses. The elevator hit floor seven and I finally exhaled. The doors opened and I elbowed my way out.

The sweet aroma of fresh coffee skated around me, a nice change from the mixture of scents in the elevator. As I walked by each office and cubicle, I was reminded of just how different my life was from even just a year earlier and how, even though I wasn't where I wanted to be yet, I was so close to living my best life I could almost taste it. It wasn't an easy transition, but I wouldn't have taken back anything I did to get me where I was.

I threw my stuff down beside my small, overcrowded desk and slumped into my seat. I logged into my computer and snatched the sticky note on my desk calendar.

Collins meeting in five minutes, conference room.

"How could I forget. Not like you remind me every five minutes," I muttered.

"Long night?" Kara asked.

"Uh, yeah I guess you could say that."

She set an iced coffee and a straw on the corner of my desk. "I kind of figured you might need a pick me up this morning, so I grabbed you one of these when I got mine. And one for Jonathan."

"Thank you so much." I ripped the wrapping from the straw and smashed it into the lid. "You ready for this thing?"

"I'll be in there in a minute."

I gripped my cup for dear life and jumped out of my chair. I took another sip and headed toward the conference room down the hall. I pulled the door open, making eye contact with Jonathan, my absolute prick for a boss.

"Noah, so glad you've finally blessed us with your presence."

"Sorry, I had a bit of a late start today."

I strode across the floor and positioned myself in the chair across from Jonathan, which I instantly regretted. Much like Medusa, it was best to avoid eye contact with him at all times. Unlike Medusa though, he didn't really seem to have a tragic back story. He was just a dick because he could be.

I set my coffee down on the oak tabletop and pulled a pen out of the binding of my notebook and opened it to a page scribbled with my notes.

The latch of the door clicked. I turned in my chair to see two women walk in. Kara stole the chair next to me, and the other, the lovely Ms. Maya Reynolds, the company's esteemed publisher, joined Jonathan at the front of the room.

"Sorry for the wait," Maya said.

"You're not late. We were all early," Jonathan replied.

"Oh, boy," I accidentally let slip.

Maya looked right at me. "What was that, Noah?"

"Oh boy, I'm just so excited to get this meeting started. Woo!"

Kara eyed me, a grin pulled at the edge of her lips.

Jonathan was probably more desperate to impress Maya than any of us. I'm not sure what he had to gain from trying to suck up to her, seeing as he was already editor-in-chief, but he would do just about anything to make sure he was noticed. That usually meant he would do just about anything to make sure our highest grossing writer continued with the company. Since I worked for him, I also worked for Cordelia by default.

"Thank you for the enthusiasm." Maya cleared her throat and turned her attention away from me. "Cordelia will be here soon. There was a bit of a wardrobe malfunction this morning during her segment for the Kaley Evans Show, so while all of that is getting handled, we'll just start."

Jonathan pulled out a black remote and turned on the projector. "*The Getaway*'s release is one week away. One week. The online buzz is substantially lower than we would like it to be by this point, so now we only have until next Thursday afternoon to get everyone talking about the book and to get it trending on all social media platforms."

"Which I'm sure is something that we will easily be able to fix," Maya interjected. "Cordelia's readers have never disappointed us with first week sales. What we need to focus on is the launch party."

I heard the door slam shut behind me and heels clacking along the floor. A cold chill rushed up my spine, leaving behind only a trail of goosebumps up and down my arms and the back of my neck. I turned slightly, glancing over Kara's head at Cordelia, who was now slumped down into a chair at the end of the table with her legs crossed.

She slipped her famous sunglasses off her face and I avoided her icy gaze. Her blonde hair hung over her shoulders.

"I'm glad you could join us," Maya said. "We were just about to discuss the launch party for the book next weekend."

Cordelia took a swig from her coffee cup, which everyone knew was never actually coffee. "I had a few comments about that."

"Anything you want."

"I hate it all."

Jonathan set the clicker down on the tabletop and looked up at Cordelia, his brow furrowed and arms crossing. "Pardon?"

"Don't get me wrong, it would be great if it was my funeral, but we need to liven it up a little bit."

"We only have a week, Cordelia. If you wanted to make changes you should have said something a little earlier," Jonathan said.

Maya gave him the side eye and he swiftly returned to his seat across from me at the table.

"With all due respect, Jon is right. At this point in time the changes that can be made are extremely slim."

"Well, it's my party and I don't want a snooze fest, which is what you turned it into with your violin players, champagne, and all of the dinosaurs you invited."

That was rich coming from someone most of us were sure was a descendant from real dinosaurs.

I let a giggle escape from between my lips and Cordelia looked at me, "Is something funny?"

"No. Nothing funny here."

The projector screen went black and Maya pulled up a chair. She yanked her bag off the floor and set it on the table, rummaging through it for a moment before finally pulling out a notepad. She let out a subtle sigh before flipping it open to a fresh page. "What are some things you'd like to add? I'll do my best to get whatever it is you want."

"I want something youthful and energetic. I want dancing, live music, and as many young and eligible bachelors as I can get."

"So, you want your own personal Coachella?" I asked.

"Yes!" Cordelia shouted. "Whatever that is!"

Maya finished writing out little notes to herself. "Alright, we'll try our best to make this night as young and fun as is humanly possible in the next week."

"Alright, it's settled. Now, if we're done here, I have a massage in an hour that I really can't miss," Cordelia said as she sprung to her feet. She pushed through the door and vanished down the hall, followed closely by Maya and Jonathan.

I swept my binder up from the table and looked at Kara.

"Well, that was fun," she said.

"Yeah, a real hoot."

I drained my coffee cup and threw it into the trash on my way back out onto the main floor. I stopped at my desk and slid my binder back into the drawer.

"I really thought Jonathan's head might explode in there."

"She's definitely a piece of work. Part of me wishes she'd just retire or something," I replied.

Kara sat down at her desk across from mine. "I know the feeling. Why does our entire financial future have to ride on her of all people? She's the absolute worst."

"I don't hate people, but if I did then she'd probably be in first place."

Jonathan poked his head out from inside his office. "Carlisle, Lynch, in my office."

"I'll be right there. I just need to—"

"Now," he demanded. He shut the glass door and returned to his desk.

I took a pile of paperwork out of my desk drawer before forcing myself up. "Duty calls," I said to Kara as we walked straight into the inferno.

I pulled the door open and we entered his lair. Just the change from one room to the next was enough to make my skin crawl. He was even more demanding than my boss at Mickey's Burgers back home, and that was saying something. I just had to get through at least a year of serving his every wish and then I'd finally have the opportunity to start editing.

I shut the door behind me and stood next to Kara.

He glared at us. "Well sit down. Do I have to tell you to do everything?"

We took a seat and I could feel my legs doing that bouncing thing they always do when I'm nervous or getting restless. I was starting to think of every possible terrible outcome in my head.

I did something bad, and I was about to pay for it with my job. I was sure of it.

I watched silently as Jonathan fiddled with a pile of papers on his desk, rifling through each one looking for some sort of dotted line to sign. I began cracking my fingers.

"Could you please not," he said.

"Sorry." I crossed my legs as he finished up writing another signature.

"With all due respect, sir, we do have a lot of work to do."

"Oh, I had no idea we were running on Kara time. Let's get on with it then, shall we? Maya, for some reason, believes that the two of you have what it takes to plan a party that Cordelia will love."

"What?" I asked.

"I was just as shocked as you are, believe me. I think it's a completely crazy plan that is sure to end in fire, but nonetheless, Maya has put the two of you in charge of all party planning."

Kara's eyes lit up. "That's amazing — wow."

"Yes, it's a dream come true. We'll check in with you on Monday afternoon to see how the planning is coming."

"Thank you for the opportunity, Jonathan," she said.

"Don't mess this up." Jonathan continued signing off on paperwork. He stopped briefly to look up at the two of us. "Well, are you waiting for permission to leave now too? I swear it's like I'm talking to a wall with the two of you."

I followed Kara back outside. "Did that just happen?"

"I think it did." She smiles up at me. "I'm so excited! I love party planning."

"I do too, but this time our jobs are on the line. Do you think they'll be happy if Cordelia isn't happy?"

"We've got this."

"If you say so."

Jonathan's words kept ringing in my head.

Don't mess this up

chapter **four**

My pen tapped against the tabletop along with the rhythm of the music blaring from the floor above.

Eventually I noticed I had been reading the same sentence over and over again for the last minute and half and threw my pen down. I glanced down at the half-finished manuscript in front of me and wept internally at the number of notes that had been inked onto the page.

The thumping and pitter-pattering of feet from upstairs continued to echo through the kitchen, making it extremely difficult for me to have a breakdown in peace.

I jumped out of my chair and grabbed the broom and began whacking the ceiling with the handle. "Hey, come on! Some of us are trying to work around here!"

The lock on the door clicked and the door swung open. Zoe walked in and stopped in her tracks. We looked into each other's eyes, my arms still holding the broom to the ceiling.

"This isn't what it looks like," I said.

"Oh, honey . . . no."

I put the broom back into the closet and slid back into my chair. I pushed the stack of papers to the other side of the table, pressing my forehead against the wood.

"Okay, what's wrong? Speak to me."

"I just don't know why I even bother writing. It's all complete garbage."

"I'm sure it's not that bad."

I yanked the stack back over and showed Zoe all of the red markings. "It sucks, and I'm a total failure forever."

"You're your own worst critic. All you can do is your best and have faith that it really is your best work."

"You're such a cheese ball," I said.

"You know I'm right, though."

I dropped the pen again and looked up at Zoe. The skin around her eyes was puffy and slightly red. It wasn't enough to notice if you weren't really looking for it, but it was enough to tell that she wasn't okay.

Unfortunately, Zoe was never the type of person to put her problems on other people, so trying to get her to admit to anything was a nearly impossible task.

She would tell me when she was ready.

"Where's Adrienne?" I asked. "I thought you were coming back together."

"Yeah, that was the original plan, but she sent me a text and said she had to stay a little longer for a parent-teacher conference or something."

"Oh." The thought rolled around in my head before I finally had to blurt it out. "So, are we ever going to talk about what happened last week or are we just going to continue pretending like nothing happened?"

She took out her phone and started playing with her case. Her eyes avoided mine.

"We can't just ignore it, Zo."

"There's really nothing to talk about."

"I beg to differ. And so would a lot of people that witnessed all of it. Did you even come back that night?"

She stood up and started poking through the fridge and cabinets. "Hey, what do you think we should have for dinner?"

She was avoiding the question, which really shouldn't have annoyed me as much as it did. I was going to eventually burst at the seams, and I really didn't want any collateral damage from the crossfire.

"Chicken marinara like old times maybe? We can all cook," she said.

"We can't just keep pretending like it didn't happen. It's making everything weird and I don't like it."

She glanced back at me. "I'll be really honest with you. I was so messed up that night that I don't remember much of anything after we got to the bar."

I wasn't sure if it was the anger from that night, or the sheer annoyance I felt from her making a scene at the bar and then avoiding me, but I really didn't believe a word she was saying to me.

She avoided my gaze and continued raiding the cabinets.

"Just . . . whatever. And make whatever you want for dinner. I have to be somewhere, and I don't have time to deal with any of this shit." I threw everything back into my bag, stormed off down the hall, and slammed my bedroom door shut.

After Cordelia basically scrapped her entire party and Maya handed the reins over to me and Kara, I was convinced we were irrevocably fucked. There was no possible way we could find another location on such short notice, which was why I was so relieved when Theo told us he was borrowing his brother's car and taking us out location scouting. We were running out of time, and I was starting to freak out.

All the locations he found were great, but as soon as the owners found out that there would be a bunch of drinking involved, they wanted us to pay a fortune. I couldn't say I blamed them.

Theo pulled up outside an abandoned building and put the car in park. "Okay, this is the last place I was able to find. Just try to keep an open mind when we get in there."

He turned off the engine and we got out.

"Oh look, there's even some graffiti. Maya's gonna love that," I said.

"Just give it a shot. Go inside, look around, and then decide. Make it snappy though. I told my brother I'd have his car back by six." Theo dug in his pocket and fished out a set of keys. "You're gonna love it. You just have to see the bigger picture." He unlocked and opened the door.

When we stepped over the threshold, I was—horrified? Yeah, that seems like a pretty good word for it.

Sure, it was huge, but there was so much trash everywhere, the floors were sticky, and there was a stench I couldn't quite place.

Kara covered her nose. "Seriously?"

"I told you to keep an open mind."

I ran my fingertips across the bar. Everything was covered in dust and the place looked like it hadn't been used in months. "I think we're gonna have to pass on this one."

"I agree that this place is kinda gross, but there's also no way we can afford the other places," Kara said. "It would completely eat away at our budget and we wouldn't be able to afford anything else."

"Yeah, but—" I wiped the dust off my fingers with a nearby rag, "this is definitely the exact opposite of what we want."

"But it's also at a fraction of the cost as the rest of the places," Theo said.

"I don't know."

"We don't really have the time to not know," Theo said. "We're only six days away and we haven't booked a new place yet. I'm friends with the owner and he's practically giving us the club. I know it's not ideal, but with the amount we're saving, we can get people in here to clean it up. It won't even look like the same place."

I tried to see the bigger picture like he wanted us to, but it wasn't easy to look passed all the dust and the trash and the stink. But we also didn't really have much of a choice. Kara was right. We couldn't afford those other places with the budget we had.

"Fine." I looked back up at Theo and Kara. "Fine. We'll take it."

"Great. I'll let Maya know we booked a place and we'll get some people in here to start cleaning."

chapter **five**

I looked down at the clock as I finished typing up the last of the itinerary for the party. Only twelve hours to get everything finalized and keep Jonathan and Cordelia happy. I felt the buzz of my phone vibrate gently against the desk.

It was a text from Bennett.

Hey, what are you doing right now?

I couldn't afford to come across as needy by texting back too quickly. Historically speaking, I'd made that mistake too many times. I also didn't have the time or patience to wait it out five minutes before replying.

Just doing some stuff for work. Gonna be a busy day. I watched as the three little dots popped up at the bottom of my screen.

I'm feeling breakfast. How about you?

I had to say no, right? There was just so much work to be done before I deserved to have any fun. That sounds nice, but I have so much work to do by tonight. *My boss will literally have my head if I don't get everything done.*

Read 9:05 AM.

I shuffled through the folder with all the information for the launch party and pulled out the checklist Maya had given us. We were both assigned a series of tasks and I had finished nearly everything.

Buzz.

Can't you spare like an hour? I really want to see you.

And then he sent a frowny face, followed by an actual picture of his puckering puppy dog face and big blue eyes. It was so damn cute. He was breaking me down.

That's totally not cool and it's unfair, I replied.

It may be unfair, but is it working?

Fine. I guess I can spare a little bit of time, but it'll be a little while, I texted. *My boss doesn't pay me enough to pay for these city cab prices.*

So just take the subway. It's faster than walking all the way here, he wrote.

You're kidding, right? I've never even been down there. The smell coming up from down there is more than enough for me. I'm not into the whole underground thing.

He wrote back immediately. *Just take the subway. It's not that bad. I take it every day and I'm still alive. Meet me by the Bow Bridge in Central Park.*

Only he could get me to take the subway after ten months of straight fear.

I quickly wrote out an email to Maya and Jonathan with the attached itinerary and hit send. I piled all my loose papers into their respective folders and threw the stack into my bag along with my phone charger and tossed it over my shoulder. As I flung open my door and ran down the hall,

I smacked right into Adrienne, nearly knocking her onto the floor.

"Dude," Adrienne said.

"Sorry, I didn't know you were here."

"What's the big rush?"

"There's just a lot to do tonight before the party. I have to run by and pick up Cordelia's dress and drop it off at her apartment, and then I have to get to setup. By the way, are you still coming? Cordelia wants as many young people there as possible."

"Absolutely! No way in hell I'm missing the opportunity to watch you have a meltdown at work." She giggled and slid her phone into her back pocket. "What time do you need me and Zoe there?"

"Party starts at nine. I'm going to try to get back here by 6:00 so we can get ready together. I need to be back there at least fifteen minutes early to make sure everything is still good to go. Nothing can be out of place tonight. My life is literally depending on this night to go perfectly."

"It'll be great. I promise everything will be fine and we will get there on time and it'll all be perfect."

"Thank you so much." I waved goodbye and headed for the front door. I put my hand on the knob and stopped. "Actually, do you have second to talk? It's about Zoe."

"Sure, what's up?"

"Has she mentioned anything to you about that night at the bar? Or where she's been spending her nights off? She just hasn't really seemed like herself."

"She hasn't said much to me at all lately. But I'm sure there's nothing to worry about. She's probably just picking up extra shifts or something."

"I think there's something she isn't saying."

"I mean, it could be. You know her though, if she wants to talk about something, she'll do it when she's ready."

"I hope you're right." I start heading out again. "I'll see you later tonight."

"Bye."

Heading out now. I'm only taking the subway for you, so if I get shanked, I'm blaming you. Be there when I can.

When I finally found the right track, I felt like one of those annoying tourists that stop in the middle of the street to take pictures. I loved the skyline as much as the next guy that came from a small town, but I was losing my patience with them.

I had to stop not once—but twice—to ask which one would get me to Central Park. The first time the lady just looked at me and walked away. The second time I asked an actual worker, and he still seemed super impatient.

I got onto the train and took my phone out, immediately turning to Instagram. It was better than accidentally making eye contact with someone. The first thing I saw, as usual, was a series of posts made by my own mother.

I regretted the day I showed her Instagram. She started posting at least ten times daily, all of which either involved her kids or photos with her newly divorced mothers group captioned with motivational quotes.

#No #One #Uses #Instagram #Like #This #Mom.

I always wondered if that was something that all moms did, or specifically just moms from the Midwest because they didn't have anything better to do throughout the day.

The rest of my Instagram timeline was the usual. Old friends from college who stayed back home in Illinois to start their families and careers, fitness models I started following after I decided really wanted to get ripped before I moved to the city (but now only followed because they were hot), and several celebrity accounts I started following due to my nosy nature.

When I got off the train, I rushed back up the stairs as fast as my legs would carry me. It felt so amazing to be above ground again. I never thought I'd miss the smells, but they were far better than the ones down there.

I felt goosebumps forming as I threw my jacket over my arms and bundled up before making my way across the greenery to the bridge. Along the way I passed several characters, including a very round man dressed up as Spider-Man and another wearing a skin-tight Iron Man onesie. Some things just can't be unseen.

As I walked passed a fitness class, I spotted Bennett sitting at a beaten-up wooden table staring out at the lake.

It hit me that it was our second date, and I had a track record of usually not making it passed the second date. I'm not saying I expected Bennett and I to end the same way, but I wasn't ruling it out either. This time I wanted it to be different, so I really needed to keep my cool, which was easier said than done.

I approached from behind. "This isn't exactly what I had in mind when you said breakfast."

"I thought it might be nice to spend the morning outdoors before it starts getting too cold. And I wasn't sure what you liked, so I just got a little bit of everything from the bakery next to my apartment."

I glanced up at him.

"You okay?"

"What? Yeah, I'm good. There's just a lot going on at work right now. It's kind of stressing me out."

"Well then allow me to de-stress you," Bennett said, leading me to the table and motioning for me to sit down. He handed me one of the coffee cups and sat across from me. He slipped two chocolate croissants out of a bag and placed them on a small plate between the two of us. "Bon Appetite."

"You really are something else."

"I try."

And he really was. It was the first time since college that I had actively gone out with a guy and enjoyed myself. It was also rare that I found a guy that I genuinely found to be extremely attractive.

Okay, I'll cut the bullshit.

Bennet was hot AF. I wasn't sure what it was that I found most appealing. It may have been the fact that he was above six feet tall, his hypnotizing smize, his Channing Tatumesque lips, or his carefree attitude. Whatever it was, I found it blindly irresistible.

"So, what's going on at work?"

"The release party for our biggest author's book is tonight, and our publisher put me and another assistant in charge of the planning because it has to be fun and youthful. The last time I checked I'm only one of those things."

"You mean Cordelia Collins?" he asked, his interesting peaking a little more.

"Yeah, are you a fan?"

"Absolutely. I've been a huge fan since *Blue Nightingale*. What's she like?"

I took a sip of my coffee. "Uh, she's—Cordelia. That's pretty much the only way to describe her."

"Man, I'd love to meet her."

"Then why don't you come tonight?"

"Come to the party?"

"Yeah, why not? I mean, I'm sure no one will really question it and there'll be so many people there they won't even notice. And you'd get to meet Cordelia."

So, I hadn't exactly told Adrienne or Zoe about Bennett yet, but I was sure they'd be able to get over it. I figured inviting him to the party would be a great way to earn some brownie points by introducing him to his favorite author.

"I don't know. Can I think about it and let you know?"

I took a bite of my croissant and realized that asking him to mingle with my co-workers, bosses, and friends might have been a little much a little too fast. I looked out across the lake and watched a flock of ducks swimming around, pecking their heads into the water every once in a while to find food.

"Oh yeah . . . for sure. The party starts at nine. I'll text you the address in case you decide you want to come."

"Yeah, that sounds good. Listen, I hate to have to cut this short. I really am having an awesome time, but I completely forgot that I told my dad I'd help him out with some yard work."

I tried to hide the shakiness of my voice. "Totally. Don't want to keep you from that."

"Thank you for understanding. I'll text you tomorrow if I can't make it tonight, okay?"

I smiled and nodded my head.

He stood up and pulled his things together, leaving me one of the extra chocolate chip muffins. I watched as he made his way across the Bow Bridge and joined the swarm of people on the other side.

He did say I'd only have to spare an hour. I was almost totally positive it was the last hour I'd ever get with him, or any other guy for that matter. How did I honestly think that would turn out any different for me? I must have read the moment wrong.

It was either that or there was some sort of curse on my dating life that prevented me from making it passed date two.

chapter **six**

I twisted my body to get a good look through the car window.

"Wait. You've been doing what now?" Adrienne asked.

"It isn't a big deal. It's only been like two dates."

"And you're just now telling us about all of this?" Zoe asked, her eyes drilling a hole into the back of my head.

"I just wanted to wait a bit and see where things were going."

In my defense, I wasn't planning on saying anything for a long while, considering every time I told my friends about a guy I somehow managed to jinx everything. College proved that. But I just had to be a giant dumbass and invite him to the party. I couldn't just have him show up and not give Adrienne and Zoe an explanation, and there was no way I could've kept them away from each other.

This was all assuming he ever planned to speak to me again.

"Well, is he coming tonight then?" Zoe asked.

"I think I freaked him out by implying I wanted him to meet my friends. He just kind of took off a half hour into our breakfast date this morning and said he had to help his dad."

"I think you're just being dramatic," Adrienne said. "Maybe he really did have to go help his dad out."

"I really want to say you're probably totally right, but I'm also a bit of a drama queen. It's kind of my thing, so just let me do me."

Zoe chuckled. "Yeah, we're painfully aware of that."

Less than a minute later, our Lyft pulled up in front of the club.

Initially I was a little skeptical of it all and I doubted that we'd be able pull off getting everything cleaned up, but I had to say it wasn't a bad location to have it. Cordelia did say she wanted something youthful and full of life after all. How much more youthful could it get than a former nightclub in Brooklyn probably swimming in bacterial infections? Sounded like a college dorm to me.

We stepped out of the car and that's when I realized the line for the party was already winding around the block. People were really excited about Cordelia.

It was either that or they were just really excited to have an excuse to drink, and that was just the people that looked like they had kids. The millennials already looked a little crossfaded. At least half of my generation was in some serious need of rehab.

Zoe eyed the graffiti covering nearly every inch of the building. "Well, isn't this charming."

Adrienne smiled. "I think it has character."

"If by character you mean Gonorrhea or the Clap, then yes, it probably does."

I led them up the sidewalk and to the side entrance of the building. "Guys, it isn't as gross inside as it looks. We've had people cleaning for several days. And I have to say we did a pretty good job getting everything set up earlier."

As I followed the winding back hallways to the main room, I felt a weight lifted off my chest. Everything was still right where it was supposed to be, which meant Kara and I might be able to keep our jobs.

I looked down at my watch. It was 8:45, so I was technically only like five minutes late for the last of final prep, but in Jonathan time that just wasn't acceptable.

"Carlisle, you're late."

I knew I should've left without the girls. "I'm sorry, Jonathan. Some stuff came up, but I'm here and I brought help." I motioned behind me at Adrienne and Zoe and their not-so-enthusiastically smiling faces.

He looked around at the rest of the crew putting the finishing touches on the party. "Kara will be here soon with Cordelia. I need the two of you to do everything in your power to make sure tonight isn't a disaster."

"Wait, are you not staying?" I asked.

"Definitely not. I have more important things to do than hang out in whatever this place is. I've only been here five minutes and I already feel like I need to scrub my entire body. Maya's going to be here later to check up on you. So far it looks like you guys didn't mess anything up, so let's try to keep it that way." He glanced down at his watch then back up at me. "Also, don't be late again. I won't let it slide next time."

I watched in awe as Jonathan walked away and found the exit. Was that a compliment from *the* Jonathan Taylor? It couldn't be. He didn't do that. I wasn't even sure he knew how to say something nice.

"So, that's your boss?" Zoe asked.

"Yup."

I heard the sound of breaking glass come from the corner of the bar, and I froze. Hesitantly, I glanced behind me and saw a giant tray of shot glasses in pieces on the floor. "And now I need a drink."

A chime sounded from the inside of my pocket. I slid out my phone and my stomach churned.

Just left my dad's place. I'll try to be there around 9:30. Looking forward to tonight. Smiley face.

Fighting a smile, I slide my phone back into its home in my pocket and nervously awaited any sign of Cordelia's arrival. Maybe the night didn't have to be a total buzzkill after all.

It's weird. Just nine months before, the thought of working a nine to five job instead of supporting myself with my own writing made me totally hate everything about the world. Yet, there I was, obsessed with the idea of impressing everyone at the company just so I could push my career further and one day get the promotion to editor.

A pair of heels came crashing against the floor like a pair of boulders. "Noah! Aye! Can you please grab this? It's really heavy!" Kara came bursting into the room, struggling to carry in a large cardboard box.

"What is this?" I asked, slipping the box from her grasp.

"Maya wanted a few copies of the book set up for a display somewhere." She leaned against a bar stool, gasping for breath. "Damn, I really need to get back in the gym."

"Where's Cordelia?"

Kara waved toward the side entrance and in came Cordelia, like she had planned some grand entrance that was thwarted by Kara's lack of strength and poor lung capacity.

"Let's get this party started!" she hollered.

Cordelia was wearing a black dress with a plunging neckline and a thigh-high split paired with a pair of black heels that had to be at least six inches. Leave it to her to dress like a woman half her age. It was her night though, so as long as she was happy, Jonathan was happy.

I dropped the box of books on the floor and looked back at Kara. "Uh — is she already drunk?"

I said it as if it actually surprised me.

"Hey, don't look at me," Kara said, "my only job was to pick her up from her apartment and make sure she got here on time. She already smelled like a bottle of gin when she got in the car."

Strike one of the night already, and the night hadn't even started yet.

The party may have been digging my grave, but Cordelia was hammering the nails into my coffin. I really did need a drink. Soon.

"Kara, can I just speak with you over there for just a sec? Cordelia, meet my roommates Adrienne and Zoe. We'll be right back."

Adrienne shot me a death glare as I tugged at Kara's arm and dragged her backstage, where the band was setting up before their show.

"What's wrong now?"

I rested my hands on top of my head. "Is there any chance that you'll be able to sober her up some in the next like twenty minutes?"

"I don't know. She's pretty out of it. Maybe if we pump her full of some coffee and force some bread or something it'll soak up some of it. She's like a walking distillery so I can't promise anything."

"Alright, you do that and I'll try to figure out what to tell the guests. In the meantime, we need to make sure we keep an eye on her so she doesn't drink anything else. This night has to go perfectly, for both our sakes."

Kara and I returned to the bar just in time to find Cordelia attempting to raid the bar while the bartender finished cleaning up the pile of smashed shot glasses.

"Okay, Cordelia. Kara is going to get you a big glass of ice water while I put these books out," I said.

"I have a better idea. Let's take shots!"

Lord, take me now!

"Come on, Cordelia," Kara said. "Let's go get you some water and see if they have anything to eat for you."

If I didn't kill her, there was a good chance Kara would've beat me to the punch. I was always a decently patient person, but something about Cordelia made my blood boil.

I glanced down at my watch again. Two minutes till showtime. And if there was anything I had learned from my time in the city, it was that New Yorkers had little patience for events that didn't start on time. "Damn it."

"Hey, it'll be fine, just point us in the direction of where you want these and we'll put them up for you," Adrienne said.

"Are you sure? You really don't have to help."

Zoe picked up the box. "We want to help. Beats just standing here."

"Thank you so much." I pointed to an empty table in the corner of the room by the front doors. "Okay, people. We have less than two minutes until the doors are open. There is a crazy line out there waiting, so brace yourselves. Everyone just have a good time tonight."

And nothing. No applause. No cheering. Not even a single smile. I don't know why I thought it would be like one of those feel good movies where people worked hard for something to finally see their vision come to life.

"Great enthusiasm, people."

I heard the approaching noise of a crowd and the music from the speakers started playing. It was going to be one hell of a night. I was just hoping for the good kind.

Forty-five minutes into the party and everything was still going smoothly. The band was finally on, no fights had broken out, Cordelia hadn't had any sudden outbursts, and everyone still seemed to be in one piece.

So, of course, I had to start self-sabotaging.

Bennett was fifteen minutes late and I was freaking myself out with every possible reason. What if his he got hit by a car? Or a subway tunnel collapsed and was trapped underground? Or worse—what if he was changing his mind about me? I was considering all the possible reasons but the logical ones.

I was a theatre kid and it was in my DNA.

I looked around. There were several groups forming into one around Cordelia to discuss the book. How they even managed to finish the book between that night and its release just the day before, I don't know. I barely had the time to breathe, let alone read a nearly 400-page novel.

Across the bar, Zoe and Kara were downing a drink with Theo. I started looking through the crowd for Adrienne, and that's when I saw him coming through the door.

Dressed in black on black, Bennett was a vision, and I knew I wouldn't be able to take my eyes off him for the rest of the night.

"You made it!" I shouted over the music.

He pushed through a hoard of party-goers and grabbed my hand. "Hey, I'm so sorry I'm late. The line for this place is nuts and they almost wouldn't let me in."

My face went hot. "Oh, I'm sorry. That's my fault. I think I forgot to put your name on the list."

"It's all good. I'm here now, so that's what matters." He glanced over his shoulder. "When you told me it was a book release party I wasn't really expecting this."

"Uh . . . yeah . . . I should have warned you. Cordelia likes things — large."

He chuckled.

"Get your mind out of the gutter. She just wanted everyone to have a good time. Do you want to meet her?"

"Definitely."

We elbowed our way through the crowd and headed in Cordelia's direction. She was busy telling the tale of her last trip to Spain where she had a month-long rendezvous with some twenty-five-year-old dude named Joaquin or something like that. It must've been nice to be able to just take off like that and experience a real life rom-com.

I pushed my way through a wall of inebriated millennials. "Cordelia."

"What do you know . . . it's my babysitter," she laughed.

Everyone else joined in with her. To be fair, she was right. That's exactly what I'd become.

At least Kara was getting to enjoy herself.

"I want you to meet my — " I paused, " — this is Bennett."

She looked him up and down like he was her next meal. It was weird how jealous I was starting to feel. It's not like I expected Bennett to ditch me for Cordelia or anything, but anyone else having any sort of remotely inappropriate thought about him made me a little uneasy.

Cordelia pushed aside her drooling fans and zoned in on Bennett. "Well, aren't you yummy?"

His cheeks turned pink and he started stuttering. It was seriously the cutest damn thing I'd ever seen. I wanted to wrap him up and never let him go.

"It's great to meet you, Ms. Collins. I'm a big fan."

"Please, call me Cordelia," she said, a devilish grin forming on her face. "Any friend of — what was your name again?"

I clenched my jaw and grinded my teeth. She knew my name. She was just being a pain in my ass. "Noah."

"Any friend of Noah's is a friend of mine. Why don't you go and get yourself a drink? My treat."

"Actually, it's an open bar, so technically it's the company's treat," I replied.

She grinned again. "Even better. Now if you'll excuse me, I need to see a man about a leg rest." She slipped between us and disappeared in the crowd.

Bennett looked down at me, his face looking a little green. "Did she just—"

"Yes. I think she did. I am so sorry that you had to hear that. I'm also sorry that I had to hear that." I let out that annoying snort laugh that I always tried to hide and knew immediately my cheeks were turning hot. "Come on, there's some people I want you to meet."

I made my way across the bar, Bennett following behind me. At the time I wasn't sure whether letting him meet my friends during the third date was really such a great idea, but it seemed like the most logical next step. They were there. He was there. The chances were high that he'd wind up meeting them that night eventually anyway.

I heard Zoe shout my name over the band. "There he is! First of all, I would like to think the both of you for helping to organize this amazing party."

Another night with a drunk Zoe. Not that I should've expected anything else out of her anymore.

Kara took a sip of whatever was in her martini glass. "Thank you."

"And was there a second thing?" I asked.

"Huh?" Zoe asked.

"A second thing. You said, 'first of all', and usually — you know what . . . never mind," I said. "Where's Adrienne?"

She continued sipping through her straw and looked around, as if she was just realizing that Adrienne wasn't actually there anymore. "I don't know. She was just here like a minute ago."

"And she didn't say anything to you?"

Although I knew even if Adrienne had said something, odds were that Zoe would have been too wasted to remember it.

I didn't know who I was more annoyed with. Zoe for being wasted again when she knew it was a big night for me, or Adrienne for disappearing during one of the most important moments of my career.

I pulled out my phone and texted Adrienne. *Hey, where'd you go? Everything good?*

Dot. Dot. Dot.

Sorry, wasn't feeling good. Couldn't find you and decided to take a Lyft home.

Well you could've at least sent me a text saying you were heading out so I didn't have to worry.

I promise I'm fine. Didn't mean to scare you. See you guys tonight. XO.

That girl, I swear.

Knowing she was safe was at least one less issue for me to worry about. Now I just had to take the plunge into very uncharted territory for me.

"Guys, I would like you to meet Bennett. Bennett, this is Zoe, Kara, and Theo."

Zoe sucked her glass dry and looked up at us, her face glowing. "Benny! What is up? I have heard so much about you."

I could actually feel the awkwardness radiating from Bennett. Or maybe I was feeling my own awkwardness and putting it on him. It was still mildly uncomfortable either way. Definitely not the first impression I wanted him to have of my friends. Maybe having him meet them at a party involving an open bar wasn't exactly the best idea.

Then again, is there ever really a great time to introduce your potential future boyfriend to your friends?

I realized using the term "potential future boyfriend" may have been a bit of a leap, considering I still wasn't sure if he'd make it through an entire night surrounded by all of the people in my life, but I was trying to be an optimist for once.

"Hopefully you've heard only good things." He smiled wide, revealing his beautifully perfect teeth, which made me feel a little more at ease. I also felt like maybe I should make a dentist appointment for a whitening.

"I promise they haven't heard *that* much."

"Yeah, he didn't even mention those extremely kissable lips. Good going, Noah. You know how to pick em, don't you?"

Foot in mouth, Zoe.

Thankfully Kara seemed to read my mind. "Okay, why don't we go get you some water, Zoe. Does that sound good?"

"Don't patronize me. I'm not even drunk and I know what my limit is."

"Oh, I think that limit was about two drinks ago. Why don't we go find some food? I think I saw some mozzarella sticks over there somewhere." Kara grabbed her by the shoulders and pushed her in the direction of one of the waiters carrying trays of food.

Theo looked at us. "Uh, I'm just gonna go make sure they don't kill each other."

"Good call," I said.

I glanced back at Bennett. His mouth was slightly open, and I was embarrassed. I was sure he was completely mortified by my friends' lack of manners. He was totally going to leave and not take a second look back. Why would he? That's probably what I would have done if I were him.

I had managed to make it passed the cursed second date somehow, but I was convinced that date three would surely be the end of it all. Served me right. I was moving way too fast by introducing him to the weirdos in my life before I was sure he was ready.

"Oh, God. I'm so sorry. I am completely mortified right now. Like that is not how I wanted things to go at all. I swear it's not usually like this. Zo's been going through something and I don't even know what's going with Adrienne right now. Hopefully you're not totally freaked out, but I totally understand if you are and don't want to see—"

And just like that, it happened.

He kissed me.

It was everything I'd been hoping for and more, which sounds like an outright cliché. It really was though. Suddenly everything left my mind and none of it mattered anymore. It was exciting. I didn't have to think about anything else but his lips and mine. I would've been freaking out over him kissing me in public if everyone wasn't already too drunk or high to care.

He pulled away and smiled down at me. "You talk too much."

"Sorry."

"You also apologize too much. Loosen up a little bit."

"Sorry. I let out a laugh. "I'll just shutup now."

A hand tapped against my shoulder. "The party looks great."

"Maya, you made it."

"I had some things I had to deal with." She looked around, puzzled. "Everything looks great, but where's Cordelia?"

"Uh, she's around here . . . somewhere." I paused. "We were just talking to her a few minutes ago, so she couldn't have gotten far."

"Oh, then you don't know her. Cordelia only needs five minutes to start a riot and shut down an entire city block."

"A city block?"

"Another story for another time. I need to find her before she does something stupid."

"You know what, why don't I help you find her." I turned to Bennett. "I'll be back in like five minutes, I promise."

I tailed behind Maya for a solid ten minutes trying to find Cordelia in the cluster of people, which I honestly thought would've been easy considering she was a total loudmouth. Nope. She had somehow managed to vanish into thin air, adding suspicion to the theory that she really was some mystical creature from the dark abyss.

"I'll go check the bathroom," Maya said. "Lord knows I've found her drunk ass in there more times than I can count. You go check backstage."

I nodded as she squeezed her way through drunk and sweaty guests, blending in with the rest of the crowd.

I made my way up the side of the stage and back behind the curtain. The smell of vomit hit me head on and got stronger the further back I went.

Lo and behold, there she was. Passed out on a couch, a drink still in her hand, and vomit on the floor next to her. There was surely a chance it was someone else's vomit. The chances were low, but it was still a possibility.

A guy can dream at least.

"I swear if the alcohol doesn't kill you I might do it myself."

The moment Jonathan got wind of it, I'd never live it down. I didn't take my eye off her as I texted Kara.

Backstage. Now.

Why, she finally replied.

Just get back here. Pronto.

Definitely one of the worst nights of my life, and that's coming from someone who got outed at senior prom.

I heard footsteps rushing in from behind me, and then a gagging sound. I was so caught off guard by the fact that Cordelia even threw up and passed out in the first place that I had almost forgotten about the repugnant stench.

"What the hell is that smell?" Kara stopped and glanced behind me at Cordelia. "Oh no."

"Oh yes. This cannot be happening right now. And Maya's here, so that's fun."

"I saw that."

I had tried my best to keep my mouth shut until then to avoid stirring up any trouble, but it all finally came out. "My question is, where the hell have you been all night? Why have I been the only one trying to make sure that this night wasn't a total train wreck?"

"Excuse me? You're not blaming this on me right now. If you haven't noticed, the party has been a success. This is just one little hiccup and something to be totally expected. I've been enjoying myself and mingling. Everything you should have been doing. She's a grown woman and she makes her own decisions."

"She was the most important part of this night, Kara. If she goes down, the entire ship goes down. It was our responsibility, as a *team*, to make sure everything went smoothly. Not just mine."

"Oh my, God! You—"

Cordelia began to stir. "Would you guys shut up? I'm trying to sleep here."

I leaned over the edge of the couch and tried not to look at the vomit. "How are you feeling?"

"I'd be better if you two would stop bitching at each other and let me sleep." She leaned back again and shut her eyes.

I heard another set of footsteps approaching from behind. I felt my body tense up in preparation.

Maya never seemed like the type of person to yell and get angry, but stranger things have happened. If anything, she was too nice, and from my experience, the nicest people were the ones to have the biggest bursts of anger. I didn't want to be the first person at the company to make her explode.

For a moment everything was silent. Maya just planted herself next to the couch, her hands on her hips, and her lips pursed. She may not have been one to show outright anger, but that didn't mean she didn't show her sass and passive aggressiveness.

"Cordelia, get up," she said.

"Just let me sleep here."

Maya stepped over the vomit on the floor and pulled Cordelia off the couch. "I'm not telling you again." She got Cordelia to her feet. "Kara, I need you to help me get her to my car. We're going to sneak her out through the back door and hopefully avoid any of the press. Noah, I need you to go out there and just pretend like everything is fine and dandy. We don't need anyone finding out about this."

"Got it," I replied.

Maya and Kara dragged her outside and I went back to join the party. As soon as I found Theo and Bennett, I knew it definitely would not be fine and dandy.

"I'm sorry. I had to take care of something. It's all good now, though."

Theo forced a smile. "So, do you want the good news or the bad news."

"I think I've gotten enough bad news for tonight, so I'll take the good news first."

"Oh, I was hoping you'd say bad news. There actually is no good news, I just thought it sounded better." He chuckled and patted me on the shoulder.

I wasn't impressed.

"Okay. Zoe is in the bathroom right now. Puking her guts out. She should probably go home."

So that's what he could have said that could make my night worse.

Zoe and Cordelia. Definitely two peas in a pod.

Of course they both had to ruin the night for me in the same way at around the same time. At that rate I was never going to get to enjoy the night. Another date with Bennett cut short by pure stupidity.

"This night literally could not get any worse. Bennett, I'm sorry about all of this. I know you came here tonight after I asked you to, but I didn't expect any of this to happen."

"Shit happens. Don't worry about it."

"I promise I'll make it up to you."

Bennett grabbed me by the hand and pulled me in closer. He pressed his lips against my head and planted a kiss. "I'll be counting on that."

"I'll get you a Lyft," Theo said.

"Thank you."

When I found Zoe, she was in the floor and had her head on the toilet seat. Her hair was covering her face and she smelled like my college roommate's trashcan after his first big party. It was actually starting to feel like she was doing it on purpose. I really wanted to hate her for ruining my night yet again but seeing her utterly helpless like that made it difficult.

"Z, are you okay?"

She just groaned.

"Okay, let's get you home." I bent down and scooped up her lifeless body. I threw her arm around the back of my neck and dragged her outside.

chapter **seven**

Monday morning wasn't pretty.

Actually, that's an understatement. Monday morning was kind of like that awkward cousin that your mom forces you to spend time with at the family reunion because they're "family" and your aunt wants them to socialize more. It was weird for everyone involved.

I found myself sitting across from Cordelia. She had a coffee in her hand and her cold eyes cut through me like glass shards. Kara and Theo looked just as uncomfortable with all of it as I did. Everyone knew why Jonathan and Maya wanted to meet with us, and I couldn't help but hate Cordelia a little bit for putting all our careers in jeopardy. If the press had seen her like that, who knows what it would have done to the company.

The doorknob turned and the door squeaked open. My muscles went stiff and I was scared to move, like maybe if I didn't show any sign of life they would forget I was there. Much like the fabled T-rex, Jonathan stalks his prey by movement.

Jonathan circled the table, looking all of us square in the eye as he passed. He circled back around to the front of the room and placed his hands flat on the table. He leaned in closer. "Do the four of you have the slightest idea how detrimental Saturday night could have been for the reputation of this company?"

Kara sat up straight in her chair. "Jonathan, I—"

"Do not speak right now, Miss Lynch," Jonathan said. "I just need you to listen." He stood upright again and slid the chair out at the head of the table. "I just hope you all know how lucky you got that no one saw what happened. I am highly disappointed in you. We thought you would be able to handle something like this."

Pardon me if I'm wrong here, but did he not say he was confused by Maya's choice to have us do the party? And did he not say it was sure to end in fire? He wasn't completely wrong about that last part, minus the literal fire part thankfully, but that's beside the point. If he didn't think we could handle it, he had every right to put his foot down. He just had his head too far up Maya's ass to go against her.

Not that it was any of my business though.

"Thank you, Jonathan, but I'll take it from here." Maya cleared her throat. "While the events at the party were less than desirable, what matters is that no one saw any of it that didn't need to. None of it got out and everything is fine."

Cordelia stood up and started putting on her jacket. "Great. Are we done here?"

"Sit down, Cordelia." Maya's voice was icy as she spoke.

I'm not sure if it was the fact that Maya had never actually publicly snapped at Cordelia before, or the raging fire in her eyes, but that was the first time I ever saw fear in her eyes.

Maybe she was human after all.

"I expect that going forward, the events of that night will never be repeated. Or I will be forced to take immediate action," Maya continued. "I will not have this company dragged through the mud. Do I make myself clear on that?"

Cordelia just nodded in reply.

"Great. On to our next line of business." Maya perked up and took the seat next to Jonathon. "I just got out of a meeting with the production president at 20th Century Fox. They read a copy of *The Getaway* and fell in love with it. That, along with the sales in just its first weekend, has prompted them to express interest in buying the film rights."

Jonathan perked up a little. "That's great news."

Cordelia shot up her hand, demanding silence and complete attention like only she could. She made me wonder how someone can get such a huge head and start thinking the world revolves around them.

"Is there a problem?" Maya asked.

"Not necessarily a problem. I just don't write with the intention of my work hitting the big screen. Films based around books never tell the full story and I don't have any desire to have my work ripped to shreds for the sake of a script."

"Cordelia, you have no idea —" Jonathan started.

"What Jonathan is trying to say is that this could be incredibly huge for you. Your work speaks volumes and no one would ever dream of defacing it."

"I'm just not comfortable with it, so I say no. If I wanted my baby to be made into a film, I would have written it as a script, plain and simple."

Jonathan let slip a subtle cough to loosen his throat and started shuffling through his pockets. He pulled out a small black remote and aimed it at the screen behind my head, revealing a bar graph about trending sales. "The release has been, without a doubt, the highest of any release in the history of the company. Readers have been so excited about *The Getaway* that the sales of your previous works have been astronomical."

"And this comes as a surprise to you?" Cordelia asked in a hushed, almost offended tone.

"This was to be expected. However, we were not expecting this large of an outcome. You've been invited to the fortieth annual Jane Dowry awards ceremony. They want to honor you with the lifetime achievement award."

"Sounds . . . riveting," Cordelia said. "I will most definitely consider it. If we're finished here, I have a very important appointment in an hour."

How was she not more excited about all of it? I would have been ecstatic about the prospect of having my piece honored like that. And to have it adapted for the silver screen? I would have gone absolutely crazy over it. It was sad to see Cordelia no longer excited about the career path she once loved so much. I guess the excitement eventually fades with everything though.

Maya turned off the screen. "Just go if you need to, Cordelia. I guess I'll tell 20th Century that you're not interested at this time."

"Thank you." Cordelia stood up again and walked out.

We were all silent for a moment.

Maya's head was titled upward, her eyes shut tightly. She took a deep breath. "We still have one piece of business to take care of. I have another meeting to get to soon, so I'll just say it. We recently had two spots on our editorial team open up, and it's my pleasure to say congratulations to Theo Reid for securing one of those two spots."

"Wait—really? Thank you so much. Wow."

"You've earned it."

She looked back and forth between me and Kara and I could feel my stomach churning.

"The two of you have proven yourself time and time again, although Saturday night was a bit of a setback, so it's been difficult to decide which one of you has earned the second spot."

I looked across the table at Kara, and by the look on her face I could tell we both had the same thing on our mind. I was obviously excited about the prospect and wanted the position. I just didn't want to have to beat out a good friend for it.

"I'll be honest and say that I knew Cordelia wouldn't be so thrilled about the idea of selling the film rights to her new baby. I've tried in the past and she just won't bite. However, I never had the two of you with me during that process."

I could see where the conversation was going.

"Jonathan and I have decided to make this running a little more interesting. The company really needs the publicity from *The Getaway* being adapted for the screen. Traditional publishing is dying, and most companies are struggling to stay afloat. That's why we've decided that whichever one of you can successfully persuade Cordelia will be the one to secure the final editorial spot."

The prospect of moving up seemed exciting, but I can't say that I knew whether it was what I could see myself doing for the rest of my life. I mean, being promoted to editor seemed like the next logical step when I was making my plans for my future.

Graduate from a good school, move to New York, secure an entry-level position, find a nice guy, work my way up to editor, get married and maybe adopt someday, and then finally work my way up to editor-in-chief or something. That was my plan, and it was all logical and safe and that's what I liked about it. I liked having definitive plans and not just winging it as I went.

But the deeper into my plan I got, the less it all seemed right and I wasn't sure of what I wanted anymore. Plus, what kind of person would I have been if I took the position from someone who I knew actually wanted it, like Kara, and then realized a year or two down the road it wasn't what I thought I wanted? I was too indecisive for a choice like that, which was the main reason why I liked to plan stuff early.

"This opportunity sounds amazing, but I think I need some time to think about it, if that's okay."

"I think I'll need to take some time too," Kara said.

"That's understandable. I'll be expecting an answer by Friday afternoon."

Maya smiled, picked up her bag, and walked out of the room with Jonathan following behind her like he was her little lapdog.

"Congratulations, Theo," Kara said. "No one deserves this more than you."

"Thank you. I honestly wasn't expecting this."

"I think everyone but you expected it," I said.

"I'll catch you guys later. I have some phone calls to make." Theo smiled and skipped out of the room.

It was just me and Kara.

"Wow."

"Yeah." She shifted in her chair and avoided my gaze.

It was still awkward after our screaming match the night of the party. It was the first time we'd ever gotten into an actual argument, but I could tell that if we went after this whole deal, it wouldn't be the last. Still, I felt bad.

"Look, about the other night. I didn't mean to blow up the way I did. I was just really tired and stressed out and you didn't deserve any of it."

"No worries. Things got intense; I can't blame you for that."

"So, we're good?" I asked.

"Definitely."

"Good. You know, I've got to say, part of me feels like I'm not really ready for the job yet."

"Don't sell yourself so short. You're ready. And if we decide to do this, we have to promise each other that there will be no hard feelings regardless of the outcome."

"Definitely. That will never happen."

I wanted to believe that would never happen, but it all gave me a weird feeling in the pit of my stomach.

I could feel the time ticking on as I clacked away at my keyboard. Every word that my brain tried to form into a coherent sentence felt like another jab at my potential writing career, which was beginning to feel like a distant dream. I was terrified to look back at any more of my previous work. There was a huge chance I'd wind up scrapping it and give up on writing all together. Again.

I heard a key slide into the lock on the front door and then the subtle click as it was unlocked. Adrienne tiptoed in, her heels in-hand, and tried to shut the door as silently as possible. She slid off her jacket and hung it up in the closet and tried not to make the floorboards creak on her way into the living room. She stopped dead in her track as we made eye contact.

"Hey. You're up late."

"So are you." I looked her up and down. She was wearing her special red dress she only wore if she was doing someone — I mean some*thing* — special. I hadn't seen it out since college. "So, where've you been all night, little missy?"

"Oh, some of the other teachers and I decided to go out and grab some dinner. Which turned into a couple drinks."

"On a school night? At—" I glanced down at the clock on my screen, "two in the morning?"

"Sometimes when you're dealing with teenagers all day you just need to get a drink on a Monday night." Adrienne threw her purse down and grabbed a hoodie off the back of one of the kitchen chairs and plopped down on the couch beside me.

"Hmm," I mumbled.

I could smell a very faint trace of cologne wafting from her dress but decided not to press on any further. Not yet at least. I didn't tell her about Bennett initially, so she deserved a little bit of time to tell me about whoever he was.

"How's the story coming?"

"It's turned into one big, heaping pile of garbage," I said, looking down at the pages I had finished and thinking about how excited I was about the book in the beginning. As time went on, I started getting self-conscious, which, to be fair, wasn't out of the ordinary for me. Normally I was able to get over that insecurity fairly quickly, but I had never gotten that close to the ending of such a long piece before.

"Come on. You're just being overdramatic. I've read some of it and it's super good."

"But that was months ago. It's devolved since then."

"I'm sure it hasn't devolved. There are loads of people who start out loving their work, then they hate it, and then when they're done with it they love it again."

"But—"

"Stop beating yourself up and just write." She leaned her head back and dangled it over the edge of the couch. She ran her fingers through her hair and then threw it up in a ponytail. "Is Z actually sleeping for once?"

"Nope. Picked up an extra shift at the ER again."

"She's been working a lot. Is she up for a promotion or something?"

There was that word. *Promotion*. It made me feel a sense of pride and competitiveness, but at the same time made me feel a little sick. I finished typing out the last of my thoughts and shut my laptop.

"Mkay, spill the beans," Adrienne demanded.

"Spill what beans?"

"Your lying face really sucks. Something is going on, and I demand to know what it is. Is it Bennett?"

If only Bennett was my biggest problem. It would've made my life so much easier if I all I needed was guy advice from my best friend.

"No, it's just work. As usual. There's a spot open for editor, and I'm in the running."

"Isn't that good news?"

"You'd think so, but I'm up against Kara for it."

"So? Crush the bitch."

My mouth fell open. Did she actually just say that to me?

Adrienne giggled. "Look, I know that she's your friend, and she's super great, but you can't worry about friendship when it's your career on the line. You may not get this chance again any time soon."

"So, you're saying even if I was competing against you, I should do everything I could to beat you?"

"Definitely not, honey. I know where you sleep, and I have access to all your food and drinks."

I scooched closer to the other end of the couch and built up a pillow barricade between us. No way I was taking any sort of chance. She was small but mighty.

Adrienne let out a giggle. "But in all seriousness, you should go for it. It sounds like a great opportunity. Do whatever it is you need to do to get an leg up on the competition."

I thought about Kara and what it would mean doing in order to get the position in the first place. Cordelia may have been completely insane, but she was also stubborn as hell. No one could convince her to do something she didn't want to do.

"Can I be honest?" I asked.

"Sure."

"I don't even know if I want it. I think about the future and I don't know if I see myself being an editor for the rest of my life anymore."

"Okay, can I just be brutally honest here?"

I nod in reply.

"I hate to say it, but there is no guarantee that you are ever going to be a published writer. There's even less of a chance you'll actually be able to support yourself financially by doing so. You worked hard to get your degree and you've worked hard to get to where you are now in the company. Don't screw it up by being indecisive, as usual."

Brutally honest was right. Geesh.

But I needed to hear that. I couldn't exactly depend on myself to kick my own ass into gear.

I scrolled through my text messages until I stopped at Kara's name. I paused for a moment and thought about all our late-night Thai takeout in the office and how different things were going to be from that point on.

I'm going for it. Hope you understand, I wrote.

chapter **eight**

I glanced down at my glowing phone screen. A text from Bennett was sprawled across the display. *Hey, where you at? I found a table for us.*

Sorry, got held up at home. Lyft is down the block. See you soon.

Ok, see you soon.

I looked up just in time to see the sign for Alessandro's come into view. The car slowed to a stop and I stepped out onto the sidewalk. The lights strung over the top of the restaurant's patio reflected off the slightly damp pavement from the snow that thankfully only lasted a few minutes. I've always had a bit of a love-hate relationship with late fall. Mother Nature never could make up her mind about anything. At least it wasn't as bad as Illinois weather where one day it's summer and the next you're in the dead of winter.

The cold air brushed up and down my skin and my body shook. I zipped my coat up to my chin, stuffed my hands into my pockets, and made a beeline for the front door. As I entered the building, I was hit by a sudden rush of warmth rushing from the vents just above me. I could smell a slight garlic aroma of a passing plate of alfredo (my greatest weakness) as I walked up to the band of hosts and waiters.

"Hi, welcome to Alessandro's. Table for one?" a young girl asked.

"Uh, actually I'm here to meet someone. I think he's already sitting down. Bennett?"

"Right this way, sir."

Sir? I was only like six years older. That's bogus.

I know, I know, she was only being respectful and doing her job and blah blah blah. I just didn't like the thought of getting older before I was ready for it. There was still so much I wanted to do before I got to that stage in life.

Anyway, where was I?

Right. The fetus—I mean high school-aged young lady—was taking me to see Bennett. I strolled along behind her to the back corner of the restaurant.

He was just sitting there, looking as devilishly handsome as ever with his cute and wavy dirty blonde hair pushed back and his blue eyes that I could see from a mile away. I took my seat and slid back up to the table.

"I went ahead and ordered you a water for now," Bennett said. "I wasn't sure if you'd want anything else though."

Order yourself wine and then water for me, huh? Okay. Whatever.

"Thank you, that's totally fine."

"I'll let your waiter know everyone's here and he'll be over in just a few," the girl said.

I took a sip of my water and looked out of the window at our view. "Wow."

"I know. This is my favorite place to come this time of year."

I glanced out to see the definition of a wonderland. The trees and iron fences outside had been decorated with white lights and were still lightly dusted in the flurries that had fallen earlier that day. I was a little pissy about snow in late October, but it was still beautiful to look at, even if I did have to wear multiple layers of underwear to protect myself from the cold already.

"It's amazing," I said.

"Yeah, you are."

I laughed. Damn, he was so smooth and amazing and beautiful. I couldn't take my eyes off him.

"So, do you know what you're getting yet?" I asked.

"That would be a definite no. I haven't been here in so long and I don't know what I'm in the mood for."

I took a deep breath and looked through the window again, my eyes tracing the winding pathway. I wanted to focus all my attention on Bennett, but I couldn't shake the look on Kara's face that morning after we both told Maya that we wanted the position. She said she wishes me luck, but I felt like I had betrayed her trust.

"Hey, are you okay? You seem kind of stressed tonight," Bennett said.

"Me? Yeah, everything's fine and dandy. I'm just—"

A broad-shouldered guy dressed in a white button down and a black tie stopped by our table with a new glass of ice water and placed it in front of me. He took out a pen and small pad of paper and looked down at us with a smile. "Hi, I'm Pete and I'll be your waiter today. What can I get for you two tonight?"

"I'm actually not sure. What's good here?" Bennett asked.

"Oh my gosh. If I told you all that we'd be here all night," Pete laughed. "Mm, but the eggplant parmesan is my absolute favorite. It's totally to die for." He brushed up against Bennett's arm with his as he bent down and flipped through the menu to his special eggplant parmesan meal.

"That does look really good. I think I'll try that out."

"It's amazing. I just *love* eggplant," Pete said. He turned to look at me, substantially less enthusiastically. "And you?"

Can I please get a big ass plate of *get the hell away from me?*

I wanted to say it so bad. You don't give one customer five-star attention and six-star horn dog, but then give their date the cold shoulder. That's a great way to find your face in a plate of fettuccine.

"I think I'll just take a plate of the Cajun chicken alfredo, please."

"Sure thing. I'll have those right out to you as soon as I can." Pete took our menus away and strolled off to the kitchen.

I glanced at Bennett who was watching Pete as he left.

"He was sweet," Bennett said with a smile.

"Sweet? He was flirting with you the entire time and being super passive aggressive to me."

"What? No, that's ridiculous."

Pete passed by again carrying a basket of breadsticks and placed it on the table. His softened eyes lingered on Bennett for a moment, only breaking away to shoot a death glare at me. I could have sworn I saw him wink too.

"I threw an extra thing of marinara sauce in there, just for you."

I looked at Bennett again and plopped a breadstick down on a plated. I took another sip of water before sinking my teeth into the garlic and butter glazed breadstick, which helped me forget about Pete for a moment.

"Okay, so maybe it's not so ridiculous and far-fetched," he laughed.

"Yeah," I said. "And what the hell was that line about him just *loving* eggplant?"

We both laughed and I tried not to let out my snorting laugh, which was left strictly for when I knew a person for six months minimum. It's absolutely terrifying and I wasn't ready to scare him off yet.

"So how was your day?" Bennett asked.

"It was okay."

"Just okay?"

My fingers fiddled with the paper ring around my napkin. "Just some things that have been going on at work. It's really no big deal or anything."

His hand touched mine and my fingertips began to tingle. "Tell me about it."

"Eh, it's nothing."

"If it's bothering you then it must be something."

I took another sip of water and cleared my throat. Putting my problems on other people was never really my thing or even something I was good at. I either didn't share enough or I shared too much. That was where I always really messed up. That and the fact that public displays of affection with another guy scared the hell out of me.

"It's just that I'm sort of up for an editor position and I'm—"

"That's great!"

"Yeah, but I'm against one of my best friends for it and I just . . . I don't know. I'm scared that it'll wind up messing our friendship up if either one of us gets it."

"Surely they'll understand if you get it, and vice versa. This isn't high school." Bennett smiled. "Besides, if you get it and your friend has a problem with it, then screw em. That's not a friendship."

"You sound exactly like Adrienne."

"Who?"

"Oh yeah, she left before you got to the party. She's my other friend. The one that isn't a raging alcoholic."

Maybe it wasn't okay for me to say that.

Sure, he probably thought I was kidding, but it was a serious issue and definitely not something I should be joking about. I'd hope that if I just continued on and didn't make a huge deal out of it, we could just glide right over it. It was the beginning of me sharing way too much.

He didn't seem to catch that part anyway.

And then it dawned on me that I didn't really know anything else about Bennett other than he was extremely attractive with a decent job. He never talked about his friends or family. But maybe that was on me. I did talk about myself an awful lot.

I took another bite of breadstick and looked back up at Bennett. "I'm sorry, I just realized how much I've been talking about myself these past couple weeks. What's your family like?"

"You know, just as crazy as everyone else's family. Mom passed when I was little, so it's just been my dad, my older brother and sister, and me for a while."

"Oh, I'm sorry to hear that."

"It's okay. I was three, so I don't really remember her. What about your family?"

"I grew up with an older sister. It was kind of the stereotypical small-town family with a mom, a dad, and then a boy and a girl."

"Sounds kind of nice and normal."

"I guess it was, but things weren't what they seemed. My parents divorced not long after I moved up here. My dad ran off with one of the women in his office and we haven't heard from him since."

"That's — wow. I'm sorry."

"It is what it is, I guess. My mom and sister are coming up for Christmas. I think you'll really like them."

Crap. I just said that. I brought up meeting the family two weeks in. Why did I always have to open my mouth and say stupid stuff? Who even does that two weeks in?

I cleared my throat and turned my attention toward the world outside again.

Bennett finished off his wine and grabbed a refill from the closest available waiter. Oh, and Mr. Eggplant — I mean Pete — brought it out to him. Shocker. I could smell what he was trying to do from a mile away.

I watched as Pete looked Bennett up and down as he poured his refill. It was like he was doing his best to be obvious about it all.

"Your food should be up shortly," Pete said with a smile. He shot me yet another death glare on his way back to the kitchen.

It was starting to get a little ridiculous.

chapter **nine**

I kept glancing down at my phone in between every few sentences of the email I was typing out for Jonathan, just hoping that Bennett would decide to text me and ask how my day was going. Things had been weird since I accidentally brought up meeting my family during our dinner date. We would still chat, and we met for coffee a couple of times, but things seemed different.

I snapped out of it long enough to write the closing. "Looking forward to hearing from you, Noah Carlisle, Hale Publishing," I whispered to myself.

I hit send and picked up my phone. Nothing from Bennett for nearly two days. I really messed up and didn't know how to fix it. So, I did the next worst thing.

I texted him. Again.

Hey. Up for grabbing dinner tonight?

I stared at my screen and felt my stomach twisting up.

Nothing.

I looked up and found Kara heading back to her desk from the bathroom. Talk about another awkward situation. We still talked all the time, but most of it was small-talk and we hadn't talked about anything other than work since I told her. The closeness wasn't there like it used to be, and it only got worse by the day.

"Hey," I said. "I'm getting a little hungry. Wanna go grab some lunch soon?"

She glanced up at me. "Sounds great, but I can't. Sorry. I'm actually eating with Cordelia today. Maya's out of town so I have to be her wing man."

Well, isn't that efficient?

"Where are you guys going?" I asked.

"This cute little bistro that just opened up down the street."

"Oh."

We both knew what was happening.

It was less about Kara doing Maya's extra work while she was out of town, and more about her getting an in to talk about the movie deal. At the heart of it I didn't even care about that. I just wanted our friendship back. She was the only person I really had to talk to in the office.

"Kara, can I just say I really am sorry about all of this? I don't want this to come between us."

My phone buzzed on my desk, causing a ripple effect in my coffee cup.

"You better get that. Might be important." Kara grabbed her coat and purse and took off down the hall toward the elevators.

I looked down at my phone again, and my heart fluttered in my chest.

I wish I could, but I have a lot of work to catch up on. I'll probably be staying at the office late.

And the fluttering turned into a stabbing.

I sunk further into my chair and glared down at my screen. I kept trying to tell myself to not read so much into it, but that wasn't going to happen. Too much of it was telling me that I really messed things up by being a little too excited yet again. I didn't know how to stop it. It was my curse.

"Aye, earth to Noah."

"Hmm? Oh. Sorry." I flipped my phone over on my desk. "What's up, Theo?"

"I just wanted to introduce you to someone. This is Henry Moore. He's the lucky guy that got my old job."

My heart stopped beating for a moment, however brief it was.

Henry had the most beautiful brown eyes I'd ever seen, soft brown wavy hair, and an amazing smile. His style was simple, but in a city filled with people constantly trying to outdo each other, it was a nice change of pace. Guys like that weren't generally my type, as I usually went for guys that were taller than me, but he sure wasn't bad to look at.

I soon realized I had been staring at him for a solid ten seconds before I managed to say anything. "Uh . . . h—hi." I began to blush.

I reached out my hand for his. He met my grasp and I felt the softness of his skin against mine. I didn't want to let go, but that would've been even weirder than the staring.

"Hi," I said again. "I'm Noah."

"Henry." His voice was soothing. "But he just told you that, so never mind. Are you an editor too?"

Sore subject, man.

"No," I said. "Not yet anyway. I'm Jonathan's assistant."

"But he is up for the position," Theo said.

Thanks, dude. Didn't really want to get into that.

"That's awesome."

There was that adorable smile again.

"It's still a maybe. We'll see."

I returned my attention to the stack of papers Jonathan pawned off on me that morning and then over to the stack of unsolicited manuscripts he decided to throw my way. It wasn't like I had enough on my plate already.

Theo looked over in the direction of Kara's desk. "Where's she at?"

"Out to lunch. With Cordelia."

He furrowed his brows. Even he knew what that meant. If she wanted to play hard ball, then two could play the game.

"So, what's Cordelia like?" Henry asked. "In person I mean."

Henry had a rude awakening waiting for him in his future. I was a huge fan when I started working at Hale, but when I met her, I was super disappointed by her arrogance and demanding nature. I expected more from a woman who wrote books with such down-to-earth characters.

"Are you a fan?" Theo asked.

"Yes and no. I'm not a huge fan, but I've read some of her stuff and I know she's got a pretty big reputation."

"Pretty big head, more like it," I muttered.

Jonathan opened the door to his office and everyone around us scattered like ants. He came closer and I could feel my blood going cold. He peered down at the stack of papers and then at me.

Pissy again.

Awesome.

He leaned against my desk and glared down at me. "That stack looks just as big as it did an hour ago."

"Sorry, I got caught up with some stuff. I promise I'll have it done by the end of the day."

"Forget it. I have something different for you to do. There's been a recent increase in the amount of social media influencers writing their own memoirs. And they're becoming best-sellers. Ridiculous, I know, but Maya wants to take a step into the future. I need you to start researching some of the most well-known influencers and compile a list for me." He straightened back up and stared at me like I was a dumbass again in typical Jonathon fashion. "Got it?"

"Loud and clear."

"Theo, walk with me," Jonathan said on his way back to his office.

"Okay, guess I'm going. Henry, you can chill here with Noah for a few if you want and I'll be right back."

Theo smiled and high-tailed it into Jonathan's office. Henry looked down at me from the other side of my desk and smiled.

Seriously, so cute. It was a nerdy kind of cute, but still cute, nonetheless.

"I could help you with your research," Henry said, "if you'd like. I was a bit YouTube obsessed in my teens, so I could probably muster up something."

"You're talking to the guy who ran a YouTube channel based around Sims Machinima videos in high school, along with a channel with my best friend, and then another channel in college." I laughed. "But I could use all the help I can get, so totally."

I stole the desk from behind Kara's desk and rolled it over to mine. Henry looked at me like I'd just robbed a bank or something.

"What? She's gone, it's not like she'll need it any time soon."

Henry smiled again and sat down next to me. I caught a whiff of his cologne as he rolled in closer for a better look. His arm grazed lightly against mine and I shivered.

He reached into his pocket and pulled out a jumbled mess of EarPods and started to untangle the wire. "Better use these. I don't want to annoy anyone on my first day."

"Good thinking."

He placed one of them into his ear and then handed me the other one. I pulled up YouTube and started scrolling through the trending videos.

"Nothing. It's all just a bunch of trailers for upcoming Christmas movies," I said. "Got any people in mind?"

"Now that you've mentioned it, I'd really like to see your old stuff."

"Not gonna happen, buddy."

"Come on. Just one video."

"No way. They're all so cringy."

He grinned and then pulled out his phone. "Fine, then I'll just have to find it myself." He picked up my name plate and turned it around to see the lettering. "Noah Carlisle," Henry said as he typed. "Found it!"

I thought I had made those private.

"You can watch it later, but keep in mind most of those videos are from like seven years ago."

"Excuses."

He scrolled through my videos and I continued searching through the trending pages for the perfect candidates. Most of my favorites, like Lilly Singh and Connor Franta, had already written and released their own memoirs, so they were out. I needed some fresh new faces, and I didn't know where to find any of them. I generally stuck to the same five or six content creators.

"I'm drowning here. Do you have an idea for someone that isn't me?"

"Ooh!" he said, his eyes lighting up. "There actually is this girl that my younger sister watches. She's only like twenty, but she's got around five million subscribers, I think. Her name is Dana—something."

I started typing away, and YouTube auto-filled the name Dana Hewitt in the search bar.

"Yes, that's her."

I scrolled through her videos. All 428 of them. Travel vlogs, covers, short films, DIY videos. Whatever you wanted, that girl probably had it. It was definitely a start.

My phone started buzzing again, and part of me hoped it wouldn't be Bennett changing his mind. I was having a good time with Henry. The other part of me was terrified that it wasn't him and I'd never hear from him again. I flipped my phone back over to see an incoming call from Adrienne. She never called unless it was important.

I pulled the bud out of my ear. "Sorry, I have to take this." I said, putting the phone up to my ear. "Hello?"

"Hey, can you talk for a minute?"

"Is everything okay?"

"Not really. I went to surprise Zoe at work with her favorite from that sub place she likes, and when I got there, she didn't really seem like herself."

"Like she was tired or something? She's a nurse, she's going to be tired."

"She'd been drinking, Noah. That's not like her to do something like that to jeopardize her job and someone's life."

"Yeah, but do you know that for sure?"

I didn't want to believe her at the time, but there was definitely a major change in Zoe's behavior. She liked to go out and have fun on the weekends, but she never drank during the week like that, let alone during one of her shifts.

"When I got there her eyes were bloodshot, I could barely understand a word she was saying, and her breath smelled like a distillery. I'd say that's proof enough."

"Well, what are we gonna do about it?"

Adrienne sighed over the speaker. "I don't know, but whatever it is, we need to do something quick before she gets any worse."

chapter **ten**

I was trying to find the courage to call a roommate meeting so Adrienne and I could finally talk to Zoe about what's been going on with her. Dealing with conflicts was never my strongest point. Especially ones involving my best friends.

We need to do it, I typed out to Adrienne. *This weekend.*

Agreed.

The door swung open and Jonathan, Maya, Kara, Theo, and Henry piled into the conference room. I knew Henry was short, but it wasn't until he was standing next to Jonathan that I realized just how short he was.

"Before we start, I want to say a huge thank you to Noah and Henry for the work they did yesterday to find some of the top trending social media influencers. So far, I've set up a lunch meeting with both Dana Hewitt and Thomas Rowland. This could be a big win for us," Maya said.

I hated the attention but loved it at the same time.

"Next on the agenda: the fifth annual Long Island New Adult Novel Convention is coming up this weekend and

Cordelia is set to appear both Saturday and Sunday for panels, signings, and a few interviews."

Another reason for Cordelia to get a bigger head than she already had. A weekend all about her. What could be better?

"Unfortunately I have to be out of town again this weekend, so I won't be able to make it. So Jonathan will take the reins on this one."

Ha! Sucker! That would make my weekend alone with Netflix that much sweeter. Jonathan would be miserable and wanting to kill Cordelia while I was at home chilling. Although, I still hadn't heard much from Bennett, so I was in for a rough weekend involving pining after someone I wasn't sure even wanted me anymore. There was a pint of ice cream and a *Stranger Things* binge-watching session in my future.

"And since we're going to be short one pair of hands and Theo and I will be busy with all the technical details, Cordelia will need someone to watch over her and make sure nothing happens like at the party."

"I'll go!" Kara shouted.

Of course she wanted to go. What better opportunity to beat me than to be alone with Cordelia for two entire days? I really sucked at the whole competition thing.

"That means a lot, Kara. Thank you. But Cordelia actually asked for Noah by name."

"I'm sorry . . . what?" I let slip.

"Congratulations, you're potentially one step closer to realizing your dream," Jonathan said. He dug a manila folder out of his briefcase and slid it to me from across the table.

"Will you do it?" Maya asked.

I wanted to say hell no.

I wasn't exactly thrilled by the idea of having to spend an entire weekend with Cordelia. I wasn't even sure I'd be able to make it through the weekend without going to prison for murder. It was a great way to get ahead in the game, though. And I'd be too busy trying not to kill her to think about Bennett.

If looks could kill I would have been six feet under with Kara holding the shovel.

"Sure. Why not?"

I heard the soft tapping of rain on the window panes begin just as I passed through the front door. I booty bumped the door closed and set my coffee cup down on the kitchen counter. I hurled the two suitcases and empty duffel bags in my hands to the floor. I stepped over them and sank into the couch.

Footsteps echoed down the hall and stopped beside me. "What the hell was that sound?"

I looked up at Adrienne. "That would be Cordelia's new suitcases and bags for this weekend. I don't know why women need so many bags if they'll only be gone for two days."

"You have more hair care products than I do, so don't even open up that can of worms. I could go all night on that ish."

"Noted."

"Why is your boss making you pick up her bags anyway? You're not even going."

"About that. She actually requested me as an assistant for the weekend so—"

"What the hell?" She lowered her voice and glanced over her shoulder down the hall. "I thought we were gonna talk to you-know-who about you-know-what."

I paused. "Voldemort?"

"We talked about this."

"I know, but I just can't pass this up. It's the perfect opportunity to get ahead of Kara."

I couldn't believe I just said that.

"I understand, but that just means we'll have to talk to her tonight before you leave." She cleared her throat and hollered down the hallway. "Z, can you come out here for a sec?"

Zoe came waddling down the hall like a little duck. She blew on her fingernails and waved them around like a mad man.

"Are you like having a seizure or something?" I asked.

"No, I painted my nails. Aren't they pretty?"

"Super pretty," Adrienne said. "Can I borrow that color later?"

"Totally. It's on your nightstand." She blew on her nails. "What'd you need?"

Adrienne poked at my side and I flinched. I was already under enough stress as it was.

"I —" my voice cracked. "I . . . I think we should all have dinner together tonight."

Zoe plopped down on the couch and put her feet up on the table. She continued fanning her hands. "I wish I could, but I actually can't tonight. I kind of have a date."

"With who?" I asked.

"It's nothing really."

"No, you cannot tell me you have a date and then not say anything else. I have to have every detail now and you can't leave anything out," I said, crashing next to her on the couch. "Spill."

"It's just someone I met during one of my shifts."

"Like a patient? I really hope he didn't have anything contagious because that's gross."

She chuckled.

Adrienne disappeared down the hall and into her room, leaving me alone to fend for myself. I had all these questions and I was trying so hard not to let them spew out of my mouth.

"No, he wasn't a patient. He brought his little sister in and we got to talking. He's really nice. Not to mention drop dead gorgeous."

I heard Adrienne's feet pitter-patting down the hall again. She came back holding a lacy black shirt and threw it at Zoe. "Here's that top you wanted for tonight."

"Ooh, thanks."

"Aye! You told her about the date before you told me?"

"Duh, she's my best friend!"

"But I thought I was your best friend," I said.

"Deal with it." Adrienne laughed. "Just promise us you'll be careful. Text us every hour so we know you're still alive."

"I'm not going to text you every hour, Mom."

"You know what I meant."

"And you're sure you're ready to move on after everything that happened with Jordon? I know how you felt about him."

"I have to move on some time, don't I?"

"Exactly. You don't have to stay barricaded up in here. You have to get back out there," Adrienne said.

"Yeah, but don't you think it's a little fast? It hasn't even been a full month yet."

Adrienne about kicked me.

"What I'm trying to say is that if you're not ready, you shouldn't feel pressured into moving on. You have to do that in your own time," I said. "

"It's just a date. I might not even go on another one. I won't know if I'm ready to move on if I don't get out there."

"You haven't even told us what happened yet," I said.

"You say I shouldn't be pressured into going out with someone if I'm not ready. But here you are *pressuring* me into telling you what happened. I'm just not ready to talk about it yet, and frankly, it's none of your damn business. I'm allowed to have my own private life."

"I know you are," I replied. "You've just been acting so different lately and we're—"

"Then why don't you learn how to respect my space and just back the hell up?" Zoe hopped up and stormed down the hallway and slammed Adrienne's bedroom door.

That went about as well as expected.

chapter **eleven**

I jolted out of bed and made contact with the hardwood. My head bounced off the floor and I felt a stinging sensation just above my eyebrow. I pressed my hand against my forehead, only to find my fingers were now coated in a thin layer of blood.

"You have got to be fucking kidding me!" I screamed. I looked up at the clock on my bedside table and realized it was only 5:15 and I was probably the only one up.

Adrienne's door swung open and she stomped across the hall. "Aye, you mind keeping it down in h—" She look down at me. "Damn, what did you do to your head?"

"My alarm clock scared me and I fell out of bed." I grabbed an old shirt off the floor and placed it against my head. "Sorry if I woke you up."

"It's totally fine. I'm usually up around this time anyway. My students wait for no one."

Adrienne helped me up from the floor and I picked up my blankets and pillows. The alarm on my phone started yelling at me again and I turned it off as I sat down on the edge of my bed and repositioned the shirt pressed against my head.

"Wait here." She took off down the hall while I continued applying pressure. She came back just a few moments later holding a first aid kit and a bottle of peroxide. She popped the lid to the first aid kit open and twisted off the lid to the bottle, dampening a small piece of gauze. "Okay, move the shirt now."

I moved it out of the way and felt the cool breeze against the cut.

"It doesn't look too bad, so you shouldn't need stitches or anything." Adrienne dabbed my forehead gingerly and the cold against my skin sent a chill through my body. She opened a bandage and put it over my cut. "Just make sure you take some of these bandages with you and keep it clean." She closed the lids to everything and sat up. "Explain to me again why I need to go to work."

"Because we all barely make ends meet as it is, so unless you would be interested in finding a three-bedroom box, I think we have to keep our jobs for now."

"Right." Adrienne made her way for the hall. "Off to get ready for another glorious day."

"Adrienne . . . wait."

I needed to get stuff off my chest. Like the fact that I had a sneaking suspicion she was seeing someone, and I knew she had a history of putting herself out there and then getting hurt. I needed to know she wasn't going down that road again.

"Yeah?"

"Uh—can you leave the bandages and peroxide, please?"

The car the company arranged for me pulled up outside the hotel. One of the only perks of the job was the occasional supply of a car service for a big event. It was probably their way of saying *yeah, we work you like a dog and no we won't pay you more, but here's a free car for one free trip to something we've forced you to attend.*

I hopped out and stared up at the twenty-five-story building in front of me. I could definitely deal with assisting the dragon lady if it meant getting to stay in such a flashy place for the entire weekend. The name *Van der Pol* was etched perfectly in curly gold letters on the metallic awning of the building.

I pulled the handle up on my suitcase and wheeled it inside, which was just as beautiful and refined as the outside. I glided across the glistening stone floor and took in everything from the meticulously placed furniture to the soothing sound of the mini waterfall pushing fresh water into a tiny koi pond.

"Breathtaking, isn't it?" I heard from behind me.

I turned around, half expecting to see a manager or owner or something.

"Dra— I mean Cordelia," I said. That was a close one. "Yeah, it's a beautiful hotel."

"I remember it before they did the remodel for a more modern feel. It was gorgeous then, but even more so now. This was the only place I would stay when I was young and here on business."

When was that? 1877?

"Thank you again, Cordelia for giving me this opportunity this weekend. You won't regret it."

"Well, the weekend is still young," she replied. "Where's Jonathan?"

"He texted me in the car. He'll be here in like twenty minutes. They're stuck in traffic."

"That's perfect. Be a dear and grab my room key and take my bags up, would you? There's a glass of Chardonnay calling my name."

I turned my back for two seconds to pick up one of her bags. "I don't think you should really be drinking—"

And she was gone, leaving behind all four of her bags. Seriously, who needs that much luggage for two days?

I slung three of her bags over my shoulder and attempted rolling the other one behind me with my one free hand. I approached the front desk and plopped Cordelia's bag down on the floor, a loud crash echoed through the lobby. I stuffed my hands into my coat pocket and dug for my wallet, pulling out my driver's license and company I.D. "Hi, I'm here with Hale publishing and I need to check in."

The guy behind the counter pecked away at his keyboard. "I don't see a — nope, here it is. We still have two rooms that need to be checked in, were you checking in for both?"

"Um there should be three rooms. Whose names are on the rooms?"

"We have the presidential suite for a Cordelia Collins, and then a single room for Jonathan Moore."

"That can't be right. There aren't any more reservations for the company?"

"Just a moment." He clacked away at his computer more. "We do have one more double room for a Theo Reid."

Sharing a room was not part of the plan.

"Has he already gotten the keys?" I asked.

"Yes, you actually just missed him, sir."

"Okay, then I just need to check in for Cordelia Collins, please."

He brought his attention back to his computer and clicked a few more times. He reached underneath the desk and pulled out a couple of key cards and then slid them through a scanner before handing them over. "Ms. Collins will be staying in the presidential suite, which is located on the eighth floor of the hotel."

"Thank you." I stuffed everything back into my wallet and into my coat pocket. I slid my phone out of my pocket and found Theo's number. I dragged all the bags back to the seating area of the lobby and dropped everything down on the floor as I hit the call button. "Theo, what's up? Was

I supposed to room with you or what? Nobody told me anything about this weekend."

"That would be a yes. It was a last-minute thing."

"Okay, you have the room keys so I can't really do anything until you come and get me."

"Already on it," I heard from behind me.

I ended the call and turned toward the elevators to find Theo approaching me, accompanied by Henry who was looking even cuter than the day before in his t-shirt and jeans. Theo had a look of contentment on his face, kind of like he was actually enjoying the confused look that was plastered across my face.

"Maya not making it, and also the addition of Henry here, was a last-minute thing, and then when they tried to get another room, they were all booked up. So now the three of us get to room together."

"And they figured they could use it as an opportunity to save some cash too," I said.

"Yup. Sounds about right."

I glanced behind Theo at Henry, who was looking around in total amazement.

"Hey, Henry."

He smiled up at me. "Hey."

"Okay, let's get Cordelia's bags up to her room before she throws a diva tantrum," Theo said.

We headed for the elevator and I braced myself for anything that may possibly come out of the weekend. I could only imagine how pleasant it would be with Cordelia involved.

I tapped the side of my foot against the leg of the table as I scrolled through my Instagram feed. Apparently Adrienne and Zoe took me being away as a chance for a girls weekend, complete with movies, popcorn, and what looked to be a homemade face mask. It was either that or they were preparing for their *Wicked* auditions.

Eventually I got bored and closed out of my apps, instead turning my attention to old texts between me and Bennett. It had been three days since we last spoke. It had been even longer since the last time we had a full conversation. He said he had a big week ahead of him for work, so he wasn't sure when he'd be able to talk.

Theo and Henry were giggling at their phones like a couple of teenagers and I wished my life could be that simple. I would've given almost anything to have an hour to just be a normal 23-year-old.

"What are you two laughing at over there?"

"It's nothing, just this video compilation Henry found. It's so funny," Theo said.

"I can send it to you if you want."

The door swung open and Jonathan marched in carrying a small stack of papers. He set them down on the table and took a seat. "Cordelia is finishing up getting ready so now is as good a time as any to have a little chat with you boys.

This weekend is crucial for the promotion of the latest title. We all know that Cordelia's last release didn't exactly get the buzz or sales that we wanted, so we have put everything we can into this."

He turned and looked right at me. I felt my heart jump into my throat.

"Her first press meeting is in an hour, and then afterward you are responsible for watching her and making sure she doesn't get into trouble before her interview with Leanne Ross at four. We had to pull every string we had to get her to do an interview with Cordelia."

"And how do you expect me to keep her busy?"

"Take her to lunch, bore her into a nap, braid her hair, I don't care. Just make sure you talk to her about signing that film deal before the weekend is over."

"Fantastic," I whispered to myself.

"What was that?" Jonathan asked.

"Nothing . . . nothing at all."

Jonathan pulled out his phone and tapped away. My phone beeped, followed by Theo and Henry's.

"I've just sent you the agenda for the entire weekend. Read it, memorize it, and live by it. Do not deviate in any way. The company needs this weekend to go perfectly and as planned."

Saturday:

11:00 a.m. — Press conference

12:00 p.m. — Lunch break

4:00 p.m. — Leanne Ross interview
5:30 p.m. — The Getaway reading
6:00 p.m. — Book signing and meet and greet
7:00 p.m. — Dinner
8:30 p.m. — Spa

"You're treating us to a spa?" Theo asked.

"Cordelia needs to have time to relax and rest up before her second round of interviews tomorrow with the Times. You and Mr. Moore will have the night off after the signing. Noah, you are to be with Cordelia at all times to give her whatever she wishes, no exceptions. Just don't let her drink."

If there was ever a time I was considering quitting my job and becoming a hobo, then that was most definitely it.

The doors between Cordelia's room and the living area slid open. She stepped out wearing a black and white pantsuit and a vacant expression like she'd been drinking since earlier that morning, which wouldn't have been surprising at all.

"Are you all ready to go?" Jonathan asked.

"Just let me find my heels, and then let's get this shit show on the road, shall we?"

I slipped my phone back into my pocket and I pulled my suit jacket back on. I escorted Cordelia to the door and watched my life flash before my eyes as I thought about the evening in store for me.

She certainly got the "shit show" part right, that's for sure.

chapter **twelve**

After the press conference, which in all honesty was probably one of the most boring things I have ever done in my entire life, I waddled after Cordelia while she dragged me along with her to the overpriced restaurant inside the hotel. I wasn't paying for anything though, so I didn't really care.

I plucked through the menu and picked something I couldn't even pronounce after I recognized the word 'chicken' in the title. After waiting a lifetime, the waiter (who also had a name I couldn't pronounce) set a large plate with an entrée the size of my palm in front of me. I looked down at my plate and felt my nose crinkle up.

"You don't look too enthused," Cordelia said.

"Uh . . . . I just pictured it being a little . . . bigger, I suppose."

"It's a French thing."

"So the movie clichés go."

I cut off a tiny piece of my food and put it up to my mouth. I guess it wasn't completely terrible, but I probably wouldn't eat it again. I looked down and realized that my tiny bite took at least half of the serving on my plate.

"Have you ever been?" Cordelia asked.

"To France? No, the only place outside of the country I've been to is Cancun with my friends in college."

"Those were the days," she replied. For a moment, she stared off into the distance, not making a sound. "No real responsibilities, staying up late without dealing with the consequences the next morning. Back in my day I was so limber I—"

"Mkay . . . moving on. Do you mind if I ask you a question?"

Cordelia took a substantial sip of her wine, which I pleaded with her not to get considering she was only hours away from a huge interview. She picked up her fork and knife and started slicing into whatever type of meat she had on her plate. It could have been beef, but I also couldn't pronounce the name on the menu or the ingredients even if my life depended on it.

"My guess is you're going to ask your question even if I say no, so go ahead."

"Why me? Why did you choose me to be your assistant this weekend?"

"Well, I would say that it was all to watch Jonathan squirm while I stole his assistant, but that's merely a perk."

I had to give that one to her. Watching Jonathan stress out about every little detail on his own was quite fun.

"But to be perfectly honest with you, you remind me of someone," Cordelia said.

"You're saying I remind you of yourself when you were my age?"

"Oh, heavens no," she chuckled. "I'm one of a kind. You do, however, remind me of my son."

"You have a son?"

"We haven't spoken in years."

"Why? If you don't mind me asking."

"Let's just say I wasn't always the nurturing ray of sunshine that I am today. I made some mistakes, but nobody's perfect."

I think I sort of felt sorry for her. She was quite possibly the worst human being I'd ever met, but I couldn't imagine what it would be like to not have anybody. I may have been far away from my family, but I at least still had my friends. All she seemed to have left was her career.

I cut off more bits of my food and tried to come up with some way to bring up the movie deal that was subtle enough to make it seem like I wasn't purposely doing it.

"Mind if I ask one more question?" I asked.

She looked up at me in silence.

"It's about the movie deal you passed up."

"I thought I told Jonathan that I wasn't interested in having my name sullied by selling it out to the big Hollywood producers."

"I mean . . . you did but I was just wondering why—"

"I will not have them ruining every detail of my work. No, sir. I've seen how they go against the wishes of all the writers I know that thought it would be a good idea, and I'm just not doing it."

"Cordelia, I get everything that you're saying. I wouldn't want anything I've worked hard on to be ruined either, but times have changed. Authors have so much more of a say in what goes on behind the scenes these days. I have seen some fantastic film adaptations of amazing books."

"Not another word."

And so we spent the rest of our meal together in utter silence.

After lunch we still had a solid three hours until Cordelia's interview with Leanne Ross. That meant I had to somehow keep Cordelia both happy and busy at the same for another three hours. Wouldn't it have been just as easy to hire her a babysitter that wasn't me?

I was relieved when she decided she wanted to spend the rest of her break time taking a nap and having some quiet time in her room. I honestly shouldn't have agreed to it, but I could only take so much of her. Who could blame me, though?

Oh, right . . . Jonathan probably could.

After I dropped Cordelia off at her suite — she for some reason felt the need for an escort — I ran back downstairs to the room I was sharing with Theo and Henry.

Before I walked inside, I could hear the music blaring from inside of the room. The sweet aroma of pizza wafted toward me as I stepped inside, which disappointingly wasn't the presidential suite Cordelia was enjoying, but at least it was comfortable.

"Y'all should really turn the music down." I eyed the two pizza boxes. "You guys got pizza?"

"Yeah, do you want a slice?" Theo asked.

"Yes please!" I shuffled to the table and yanked a huge slice of pizza out of the box. I was so hungry even after the super filling lunch.

"She made you go to one of those restaurants with the tiny portions, didn't she?"

"Yep. I can't tell you how good this tastes right now."

As I was stuffing my face, Henry walked out of the bathroom. "Hi."

"Hey." I took another chunk out of my pizza and savored every second of it. I probably shouldn't have been as in love with that pizza as I was in that moment.

"Not to interrupt this riveting conversation or anything, but where is the dragon lady anyway?"

"The dragon lady?" Henry asked.

"Long story," I said. "She's taking a nap before the interview later."

"Are you sure that's such a good idea? I mean, I'm relieved to not have to deal with her anytime soon, but should she really be alone?"

"We made sure room service took all of the alcohol out of the mini bar, so it should be fine," I said, stuffing the rest of my food into my mouth.

"And you guys checked all of her bags to make sure she wasn't storing anything?"

"Uh . . . no . . . was I supposed to?"

"I guess not, but it would've helped. I remember one time she smuggled three bottles of wine and a bottle of tequila onto one of these trips. It could have been a huge disaster if we didn't find her in time."

"I'm sure it'll be fine. She just wanted to take a nap. She did seem super tired."

He looked down at his watch. "I have to meet with Jonathan and go over some details for tomorrow. Feel free to just hang out and relax, but make sure Cordelia is up in the next hour. She can't miss this interview."

Theo was starting to sound like a mini Jonathan. Maybe it was something that came with being an editor. Or something that came from working so closely with someone who put the 'i' in prick.

"I got this."

I finished eating and crashed onto the bed. It was so exhausting waiting on Cordelia hand and foot and all I wanted to do was sleep for the next week. What I wouldn't have given for a vacation. I sat up and kicked my shoes off. "So, tell me all about Henry Moore."

He looked up from whatever he was playing on his laptop. "What do you want to know?"

"Everything. Where are you from? Where did you go to college? How many siblings do you have?"

"Well, I grew up in Illinois, and then we moved here my freshman year when my dad got transferred for work. I graduated from NYU last year."

"Hey, I'm from Illinois too. You're the first person I've met here that wasn't already from here."

"Really? I've met a lot of people here that were from Illinois. Although they were usually from Chicago, which might as well be its own state."

"Right? They live in their own little world up there. Every time I tell someone I'm from Illinois they assume I mean Chicago."

He laughed and it was an amazing sound. "They all suddenly lose interest when I tell them I grew up with cornfields."

It was nice meeting someone who understood where I was coming from. I had Zoe and Adrienne, but they were busy with their own things most of the time. At least with Henry I had someone at work I could talk to. Kara wasn't really an option anymore.

"Dude, your head is bleeding."

"What?" I put my fingers up to my head where the bandage was covering the gash and felt a small of trickle of blood. "Crap. Can you get into my bag and grab the bandages and antibiotic ointment please? It's the red one." I grabbed some tissues from the bed side table and tried cleaning up the blood rolling down from my forehead.

Henry opened the box of bandages and set it down beside me. Then he dashed off to the bathroom and returned with a wet washcloth.

"Thank you."

"Here, let me help you." He dabbed at my forehead and I winced. "Sorry."

"No, it's okay. It hurt worse this morning."

"How'd it happen anyway?"

"Uh, it's a long story."

Yeah, I fell out of my bed. The end. It was too embarrassing to say out loud.

When he was finished wiping away the blood, he opened the ointment and used a tissue to dab it on. We locked eyes and I could feel his breath against my face. There was a fluttering in the pit of my stomach and my heart started racing again. He probably wasn't into me though. I didn't even know if he was gay or not. It's so awkward waiting around and looking for signs, and it's even worse just downright asking them.

It wasn't like Bennett was actively pursuing me anymore. I felt like I was doing most of the work.

"You're really good at this."

"When you're as clumsy as I am, you kind of have to get really good at medical care," he said, grinning.

"Well, I'm sure your girlfriend appreciates it."

Yup. I did that. I tried to fish it out. The worst type of person. It made me feel a bit like of one of those older gay predators you hear about all the time that give the community a bad name.

"Actually, I don't have a girlfriend right now. I just got out of a bad relationship a couple of months ago.

"Oh," I said. My voice cracked a little bit. I wanted an answer. I just really hoped it would be one I liked a little bit better.

He tore open a bandage. "It's not that I'm not looking still. I guess I just haven't found the right girl yet." He looked me in the eyes again. "Or guy."

"Oh." It suddenly got a little more difficult to breath and my palms were sweating. "I guess I haven't either." I paused. "With the right guy I mean. Or maybe I have. I don't know. It's complicated. And I just keep talking. I'm sorry. And I'm still talking. I gonna stop talking now."

He scooted closer and the hairs on the back of my neck stood up. I was technically still going out with Bennett and I felt like I needed to know where we stood, so I felt bad for wanting it to go somewhere. But at the same time, I wasn't even sure if Bennett was right for me at that point in both of our careers. We were both so busy all the time and I hadn't seen much of a sign that he still wanted to go out.

I opened my mouth to say something and avoid the situation, but nothing came out. His arm brushed up against mine and I just sat there like an idiot. I swore if my heart started beating any louder, he would have heard it.

My phone started buzzing in my pocket. I pulled it out and pressed answer, still staring into Henry's golden-brown eyes. "Hello?"

"Hey, you better get to Cordelia's suite," Theo said on the other line.

"What?" I asked, not quite sure I heard him right.

"Get here quick. It doesn't look good."

I had one job and I couldn't even do that right.

One damn job!

chapter **thirteen**

It was like a bad car accident. I wanted to look away, but it was close to impossible not to look. I wasn't sure whether or I should laugh or be worried.

I walked in to find Jonathan and Theo standing around Cordelia, who was passed out on the floor. She had an empty bottle of wine in one hand and a half-eaten sandwich in the other hand. Somehow, she had managed to smear her lipstick up her cheek and her eyeliner was dripping so bad it looked like she'd gotten into a fight and lost.

"I told you to do one thing all weekend," Jonathan shouted. "One thing! How hard is it to look after a grown woman and make sure she doesn't do something stupid?"

If this had been my friend it would've been a Snapchat story just waiting to happen, but I figured that wasn't appropriate in the situation.

"Are you even listening to a word I'm saying right now, Carlisle?"

"Yes. I am. And I am sorry that I left her alone. She said she wanted to take a nap. I didn't think anything of it."

"Of course you didn't. Why would you? You never think about your actions and how they affect other people. If this whole thing goes south, it'll be on you."

"Hey now," Theo said. "There's no need to start turning on each other like this. Cordelia made her decision. This had nothing to do with Noah. She's a grown woman."

At least someone had my back.

Jonathon let out a huff and crossed his arms. "Carlisle, make yourself useful and go grab her a cold washcloth."

I found the bathroom and stuck a washcloth under the fountain of cold water. I knew that what happened wasn't totally my fault, but I still felt responsible for it all. I not only managed to irritate Cordelia more by bringing up the film rights, but I also potentially sabotaged the company's reputation and ruined the entire weekend. I was on a roll.

Jonathan and Theo were trying to get Cordelia off the floor and back on her feet when I made it back. I handed the washcloth over to Theo and he started patting her face with it.

"Cordelia, come on. Let's get up," Jonathan said. "How much did you have?"

"I don't—I—" she mumbled.

Jonathan snatched the washcloth out of Theo's hand and started wiping the smeared makeup off her face.

Cordelia had been drunk around me before, but I'd never seen her that far gone. Most of the time she was at least partially conscious and capable of pulling herself together. I was getting scared she wouldn't even make it through the day. Jonathan looked down at his watch. Only a little over an hour until the interview, so it was too late to cancel, but there was no way she'd be ready for it in time.

"This is a disaster."

"I can fix this," I said. Or at least I hoped I could.

Jonathan furrowed his brow. "And how do you expect to do that?"

That was a good question, but if I could handle Zoe at her worst, I was sure I could handle Cordelia.

"We're going to need lots of black coffee, a ton of water, and someone needs to shovel some bread into her to help soak up some of that wine."

I didn't know if any of it would work, or if an hour would even be enough to do it. But I had to hope.

It was a disaster waiting to happen. I couldn't look. I was going to ruin Cordelia's reputation, the reputation of the entire company, and everyone was going to lose their jobs and have to live out in the streets.

It was all going to be my fault.

I stood in the corner of Cordelia's suite watching as the crew finished setting up the cameras for the Leanne Ross interview. Not a job I would want to do. My anxiety was at an all-time high just knowing that whatever happened in the next ten minutes could potentially make or break my entire career.

I started gnawing on my fingernails in anticipation of Cordelia coming around the corner from the bathroom with Jonathan and an entire army of hair and makeup artists. At any second my world could have come crashing down. There was no way Jonathan or Maya would even consider me for the position if I couldn't manage to get Cordelia through the weekend in one piece. I'd be lucky if they still let me be an assistant after all of that.

Theo and Henry were both oddly calm and sitting in another corner of the room. Theo nodded his head in the direction of the bathroom and my heart stopped. They were coming, and I wasn't ready. It was like a form of sleep paralysis. My breathing found a rhythm again as Jonathan and Cordelia came into sight.

Cordelia seemed extremely put together for someone who was practically in a coma not even an hour earlier. Her hair and makeup were back in place, she was walking straight, and she was conscious, which was a miracle in itself. I loosened my fists and realized I'd been digging what little bit of nail I had left into my palms.

"Good thinking on your feet," Theo said.

"Don't celebrate just yet, Carlisle. She still has to make it through the interview."

Funny how Jonathan's support didn't make me feel any better.

I watched Cordelia and Leanne finish up last minute camera tests and go over the questions that would be asked during the interview. That's the part I never knew about until I joined the team. It makes sense though. Wouldn't want any surprises or scandals starting. Not that Cordelia needed any help in that department.

The red light of the camera came on and I felt nauseated.

I was amazed by how composed Cordelia was. Legs gracefully crossed, attitude in check, and for once all smiles. She'd been trained to compartmentalize her public image and her personal life. Well, when she wasn't wasted at least. She almost seemed kind of sweet.

"So, you've been in the business for quite some time now, and I won't say how long because I can't age you without aging myself," Leanne laughed. "Do you still get nervous right before a big release like this?"

Cordelia smiled and followed up on Leanne's laugh. Nice touch. "Yes, I can definitely be categorized as a literary vet, but still even now I get extremely anxious before I release anything to my readers. Especially with *The Getaway*. It is so much different than anything I've written previously."

"I just want to say that I've been obsessed with your work from the very beginning. I don't think I've ever missed a release. As I was reading through this one though, I did notice that it was much darker than anything else you've released. Were you worried at all that it would affect sales or that your readers wouldn't respond as positively to it?"

"Well thank you so much for saying that. I appreciate it," Cordelia said. She took a deep breath and I thought I saw a slight twitch of her eye. "And it's always something that's feared by anyone who works in the arts or entertainment business. A lot of the time we're told to stick with a specific brand because that's what sells and what an audience knows and expects, but I think I'm at the point in my career where I should be changing things up and finding what I want to write about now versus what worked for me when I started."

Cordelia started subtly repositioning in her chair and breathing a little heavier.

"And where did the spark for the story come from? As you're reading, the dynamic between Paige, Beck, and Andy seems so real and emotional. You can't help but feel like it's coming from a raw place."

Cordelia took another deep breath in. Her sweat was starting to shimmer under the studio lights. "Well, it came from a—it all started with—I—"

It was happening. It was all happening and there was nothing that I or anyone else could for her anymore.

"Are you feeling okay, Cordelia?"

"Hmm? Yeah, I'm gr—oh, God. Oh no—" Cordelia jumped out of her seat and high-tailed it to the bathroom.

There was the other dropped shoe that Jonathan had been waiting for.

I swore he was actually rooting for me to lose everything.

chapter **fourteen**

I was beginning to notice something. Every time I stepped into the conference room at work, I walked out feeling much worse than I did when I walked in. Therefore, I started to associate the conference room with anxiety and a deep funk.

"There are so many things that I want to say to all of you right now. Unfortunately, HR frowns on everything that I would like to say. However, what I can say is that if it were up to me all three of you would be *fired*! How do all of you manage to let a weekend that was supposed to be simple and uncomplicated become one big, fuc—"

Maya walked in and set her bag down by the door. "Okay, Jonathan. That's enough. Sit down."

Jonathan kept his feet planted to the ground.

"I said sit. Now."

I think I saw him roll his eyes as he pulled out his chair and sat down. His brow was still furrowed and his nose crinkled.

Maya stood at the front of the room and scanned us all.

I sat in my chair, my legs bouncing up and down, browsing Theo and Henry's expressions. The look in their eyes said it all. They were just as terrified as I was. Even worse, Cordelia walked in holding an iced coffee and wearing a pair of sunglasses, obviously still reeling from another night with her favorite man, Jack Daniels. That woman needed help.

"Oh, how great of you to join us, Cordelia. I hope we didn't disturb your very busy schedule," Maya said.

Not a peep.

"Saturday was . . . how do I put it delicately? Oh, it was a damn train wreck. A train wreck straight from Satan himself." She stopped and readjusted her jacket. "I'm not gonna yell at you. That won't accomplish anything. But I am disappointed in everyone in this room. And I do mean everyone." She eyeballed Jonathan. "I've known Leanne for years, and she's no idiot. I told her Cordelia caught food poisoning, but it was obvious by the pure vodka and wine dripping from your damn pores what was really going on."

Maya stopped again and looked directly at Cordelia. Still no reaction. I wasn't even sure her eyes were open behind those sunglasses.

"But because I have known Leanne for as long as I have, she has decided to let us have a do-over interview on Friday morning at the studio."

Great. Another chance for Cordelia to ruin everyone's lives by getting drunk and vomiting everywhere. This time in front of a live studio audience. I couldn't wait.

"And if you don't show up as sober as the day you were *born*, Cordelia, I have no choice but to let you out of your contract. I'll let you be someone else's problem."

Yeah. She said that. Word for word. Everything was verbatim. It was getting real.

Cordelia removed her glasses. Her eyes were puffy and the circles under her eyes were beyond being fixed by any type of concealer. I'd been through a hangover before, but she took it to an all new level.

She turned her head and looked Maya square in the face. "You wouldn't do that. You need me, and you know you do."

Maya placed her palms flat on the table and leaned forward. "But, that's where you're wrong, Cordelia. We need a good writer. Someone who has a way with words and can captivate an audience. We may need the talent, but we don't need *you*."

Cordelia's hands started to shake a little. The first time she'd ever visibly shown a real sign of weakness. "You're bluffing."

She leaned in closer. "Try me, sweetie." Maya stood up again and grabbed her bag from the floor. She looked at all of us one last time and then left everyone just awkwardly staring at each other in silence.

Jonathan was the next to leave, then Cordelia, and then Theo and Henry. I stayed back for another moment trying to process everything that had happened.

Surely Maya couldn't have been serious about dropping Cordelia. She was like the Beyoncé of the publishing world, and nobody would dare fire Beyoncé, let alone *threaten* to fire her. She was one of the publishing house's original big-name writers and basically helped put Hale Publishing on the map.

I finally finished collecting my thoughts and headed back out to my desk. As I started going through the dozens of emails Jonathan had sent me with instructions for tasks that he could have easily done in two minutes tops, I kept getting the sensation that someone was burning a hole into the side of my head. I glanced up from my monitor and made eye contact with Kara, who wasn't even trying to hide her smirk.

"Is there a problem?" I asked.

"Nope. No problem at all. I just heard you had quite the eventful weekend."

"Yeah, it was kind of crazy."

"A little more than *kind of* from what I heard. I just think it's funny how you're practically handing me the win here."

"Excuse me?"

"Come on, Noah. You've basically been put in charge of two events, and both times you managed to royally screw it up. If I were you, I'd give up while you still have a job. You might not be so lucky next time."

Before I knew it, I found myself walking toward the front doors of the school where Adrienne taught with some double cheeseburgers, a large fry, and a couple of chocolate shakes.

I had to get out of there for a while before I strangled Kara. I was planning on grabbing a quick snack and just working through my lunch break, but the thought of having to even be near Kara for longer than I had to felt dangerous. I had no idea she would turn into such a massive pain in my ass when in a competitive state. I needed a little best friend time to get my thoughts straight.

The first set of locked doors buzzed open and I walked into the main office. "Hi, Caroline."

Lunches with Adrienne used to be more of a regular thing before life started happening.

"Noah! It's been too long."

"I know. Work's been crazy, so I haven't really been able to get away much. Thought I'd surprise her during her lunch hour." I signed in and took a visitor pass.

"Oh, that sounds lovely. Enjoy your lunch."

I reached into my bag and pulled out an extra burger. "Don't think I forgot about you though."

"Thank you. You're the best."

"I try. Enjoy your food and try not to let these teenagers get to you too much."

I felt bad for Caroline. She was an amazing person with the biggest heart working in a school filled with a bunch of ungrateful little brats. I even saw a couple of the kids yelling at her one day. She didn't deserve any of the verbal abuse. Made me want to adopt her as my own grandma.

It was lunch time for some of the kids and I couldn't believe some of the conversations I overheard on my way down the hall passed the cafeteria. Made me wonder if I was that annoying and melodramatic in high school.

Each and every one of them were going to be knocked on their asses once they hit college and the topic of who was dating whom would be the least of their problems.

I had a huge amount of respect for Adrienne and anyone else who decided to return to high school to teach the next generation. I almost joined their ranks, but after I stopped to think about the fact that teachers get crap for pay, I decided on another route. That and the fact that high school was a complete nightmare and I couldn't handle it the first time, let alone from the time I graduated college up until the time I would be able to retire, given that retirement would still be a financial option by that point.

My stomach growled and the smell of the bacon from my burger was seeping from the bag. I knew she'd probably be at her desk eating one of those frozen meals while grading papers. She called them efficient. I called them a crime against humanity. So gross.

I pulled the door opened and tip toed inside. I could smell the food and feel my mouth starting to water. I opened my mouth to talk but stopped dead in my tracks.

So that was what she was hiding from me. There. Right in front of me. Adrienne sitting on the edge of her desk.

Making out with another teacher. Or at least I hoped it was a teacher. He was wearing dressy clothes, so I could only assume he was.

I backed out slowly and made my way back outside.

I set the food down on a bench and dug in my pocket for my phone. I scrolled through my messages and stopped at Bennett. Something told me Adrienne would be busy all night again and who knew what Zoe would be doing or if she would even be willing to talk to me.

Drinks tonight?

I wasn't sure what I expected, but I definitely didn't expect him to reply as fast as he did. Maybe he wasn't losing interest after all.

Sure, sounds fun.

chapter **fifteen**

The air whipped against my skin. It wasn't cold enough yet to cause any pain, but I could feel my face starting to numb. Based on the subtle pink shade of Bennett's cheeks, I could tell he was feeling it too.

Bennett's hand brushed against mine, causing the jerk reaction of moving my hand out of the way. He led me down the block into this little shack of a bar I would have missed had I been out walking on my own. The smell of fried food and beer hit me like a truck and my stomach started growling. It kind of reminded me of home. It also reminded me of the many reasons I wanted to leave the Midwest in the first place.

We found an empty table next to the bar.

"How'd you find this place?"

"It was a long night with some friends. That's all I'll say. I can't have you thinking I'm an alcoholic or something."

I laughed. "Well I guess tonight will tell."

Bennett strolled over to the bar and bought us both a drink. It was weird being there. I was so used to meeting at places where things were on my terms. Roles were now reversed, and I felt a little out of my element. But it was also kind of nice not being in control for once.

He set some weird brown drink down in front of me and I made the mistake of smelling it. "What is this?"

"Just something my buddy over there created. Just try it."

He took a sip and I just stared at him as he let it glide down his throat. I wasn't sure if I was going to drink it. I'd had some messed up stuff in the past, but whatever it was didn't really look all that—safe? The amount of whisky I smelled was probably enough to get me drunk in five minutes.

"A little chatty with the bartender I see. You must come here often."

"I mean, I guess I've been here a few times. I live down the block actually, so it's efficient."

"Oh, so you *are* an alcoholic, then?"

Bennett flashed that million-dollar smile. "Ah, you caught me." He took another sip from his glass. "You ever play pool?"

"Sort of, but I'm not really very good at it."

"Well, drink up and follow me."

I took a deep breath, put the glass to my lips, and tilted my head back. Whatever it was burned all the way down my throat, and I tried not to throw up when it hit my stomach.

"There ya go!"

"Oh, God. That's horrible."

"I never said it wasn't. But it's strong and budget-friendly. Let's go play some pool."

Bennett led me to the other side of the bar to the couple of pool tables they had and handed me a cue stick and chalk. I watched him chalk up his own stick and tap off any extra dust at the end of it. I had little to no idea what I was doing so I copied whatever he was doing.

He watched my every move and laughed. "Something tells me you've never actually played pool before."

"I've played with my sister at one of the bars back home before. Just out of boredom. I didn't know what I was doing though."

"Well then allow me to demonstrate." He placed the weird triangle thing at the center of the table and started throwing in all the balls. "So, the first thing you want to do is make sure that the 8-ball is in the middle when you rack up all 15 balls."

"And does it matter how you do it?"

"There's really no one way to do it. You just always need to make sure that the 8-ball is in the middle like this." He finished lining up all the balls and removed the triangle. "Next what you're gonna want to do is break, which is the first shot where you hit all 15 balls with the cue ball."

I kind of already knew that part, but I liked hearing him say it. I liked hearing him talk, period.

He bent down over the table and lined up his shot. I watched intently as he brought the stick back and the balls scattered across the table. One of the solids went flying into one of the pockets.

"Well, I guess I'm solids." Bennett smiled again and stood up straight. He tried for another shot and missed. "Your turn."

I leaned over the side of the table and kept my eye on of the stripes close enough to a pocket for me to hit. I tried to hold the cue stick and take my shot, but that didn't really go so well. "Told you I wasn't very good."

He chuckled and shook his head. "Here, let me give you a hand."

He came up behind me and I felt his breath against my neck and his chest brush up against my back. "Are you right handed?"

"Yes."

"Okay, so what you're gonna want to do is hold the base of the stick with your right hand and then grasp the top with your left."

I laughed. "We still talking about pool here?"

I couldn't see him, but I could tell he was probably grinning from ear to ear.

"So, now curve your left index finger over the top and then your thumb underneath like this." He put my hand into position and put his hand around my wrist. He guided my arm back. "Focus. Bring it back and then—" He knocked the stick against the cue and the ball I was aiming for rolled into the pocket. "And that is how you play pool."

"I feel like you've been planning this."

"I can't say I know what you're talking about. I have done no such thing."

"Right. Bring me here, I don't know how to play pool, and then you come up behind me and put your arms around me to show me how to play. Totally not planned or anything."

He edged closer and brushed his hand against my cheek. I looked around and noticed some of the bar's patrons staring. I backed away and sat against the edge of the table.

"You're up," I said.

He laughed and grasped his pool stick tighter.

"I mean, it's your turn."

I desperately wanted to feel comfortable with PDA, but it was nothing but a source of anxiety for me. Growing up in a smaller, more conservative town just made me scared of publicly showing who I was. It was something that stuck with me through life and probably something that will never actually leave. I didn't want to be one of those people you read about in the news after they were a victim of a hate crime.

A group of voices rang out from across the bar. "Benny!"

I turned and saw two guys and a girl heading our way.

Bennett perked up in the middle of aiming for his next shot and whipped around. "Hey!"

"Didn't expect to see you here," one of the guys said.

"Yeah, you've been holed up so long I was beginning to think you were dead or something," another guy said.

Bennet set his cue down on top of the table and gave all three a hug. "Sorry, I've been busy with work and stuff."

The girl locked eyes with me. "And who's this?"

"Uh . . . hi," I stuttered. "I guess I'm the stuff."

"This is my friend Noah. Noah, this is Jake, Lawrence, and Clarisse."

His friend?

Fair enough. It wasn't like we'd had any sort of serious talk about what we were or where things were going.

"It's great to meet you, Noah," Clarisse said. "I have to say you picked a cute one this time, Benny."

"Benny?"

"It's a long story," Bennett said.

"One that I would be more than happy to tell you all about. We were gonna have a few drinks and some cheese sticks. You guys care to join us?"

"We were actually just about to leave," Bennett said. "Maybe next time though."

"Oh, okay. Text me later?" Clarisse asked.

"Definitely." Bennett grabbed my hand and pulled me out of the bar and down the street.

I wasn't sure if I should feel offended or not. I knew people took their own time with everything, but he rushed me out so fast my head was spinning. We walked in silence together down the street. I zipped my coat up to combat the dropping temperatures and watched Bennett's face as we walked. His lips were tucked into his mouth, and he looked a little pissy, but also confused.

We stopped outside an old brick building.

"Where are we?" I asked.

"This is my place. Hope you don't mind."

"No. Not at all."

He unlocked the building's main entrance and we got into the elevator. He pressed floor four and the doors closed.

"So, can I ask you something?" I asked, leaning against the handrail.

"Sure."

"Why exactly did we run out of there so fast? I wanted to get to know your friends."

The elevator stopped and the doors opened. He stepped out and walked down the hall. I followed. We stopped in front of 4E and he slid his key into the lock. There was a subtle click and the door swung open. He led me inside and into the living room where he took off his coat and laid it down on an armchair. "Take off your coat. Stay a while."

I slipped my coat off and put it next to his and joined him on the couch. "You still haven't answered."

"Look, it's not that I don't want you to meet my friends. It's just that I—I don't really like hanging around them. We were all in high school and college together and they were great, but one day I grew up and they didn't. They're into drinking and partying and I'm just not into that life anymore."

Good excuse. Never heard that one before.

"So you're not embarrassed of me?" I asked.

"Embarrassed? Yes. Of you? No."

"What are you embarrassed of?"

"Just that I knew them in the first place. And of who I was."

"You don't seem too bad now from what I can see."

He leaned in and I felt his warmth radiating from beneath his white tee. He grazed my cheek again with his hand and it was like I was under some sort of spell. His hand wrapped around the back of my neck, and he pulled me in closer. My knees trembled when his lips locked with mine. He pulled back and looked me in the eyes.

"Wow."

"Do you maybe wanna take this into my room?" he asked, almost in a whisper.

"Sure."

He grinned at me one last time before leading me into his bedroom. The door shut softly behind us and his arms wrapped around me, pulling me in close. His lips caressed mine before trailing up my neck, leaving behind small kisses as we went.

chapter **sixteen**

I crept inside, making sure my boots didn't make too much noise on the old floors.

I hung my keys on the hook beside the door and returned my coat to its home in the closet. I kicked off my boots and rummaged through the fridge for a snack, finding a piece of pizza someone wrapped up in foil to be forgotten about until the next stress cleaning.

A rustling lingered from behind me. Turning back, I found Adrienne hovering over me with a baseball bat ready to pounce.

"Holy shit! Why do you have a bat?"

"I thought you were a burglar!"

"So, you choose to attack instead of calling the police?"

She lowered the bat and used it as balance support. "Bitch, I'm from the south side of Chicago. If we waited for the police, we'd all be dead. Besides, I'm not afraid of a little food snatcher.

Adrienne swung the bat over her shoulder, and I followed her into the living room with my half-eaten slice. We nestled into the couch where I finished my food.

"Where've you been?" she asked.

"Nowhere."

"You're a terrible liar."

"I may or may not have been at Bennett's place."

Adrienne grabbed her phone from the table. "Uh, since you got off?"

"Not the entire time. We went out for drinks and then we wound up back at his place."

"And did you guys—you know—"

I threw a pillow at Adrienne's head.

"What? I'm just asking." She laughed. "You really like him, don't you?"

"Yeah, I really do. But—"

"But?"

I rested my head on her shoulder. I was sure she'd just tell me I was overreacting again. It's what I did best. "But . . . I don't know. I know it's gonna sound really whiny, but earlier we ran into some of his friends and he wouldn't even fully introduce me or let me talk to them. He just said I was a friend and then said we had to go."

"Well maybe he just wants to wait a while before he starts introducing you to people in his life."

"That's what I thought too. When we got back to his place, he told me that they weren't really his crowd anymore, which I understood, then we wound up—you know—but then he basically pushed me out of his apartment when he was ready to just sleep."

I wanted some words of wisdom and for Adrienne to tell me I was just overthinking everything, which I did a lot. Instead, she just gave me the look. You know, the one where you know that you're thinking the same thing, but neither one of you really wants to admit it.

"Okay, you can say something at any point," I said.

"Do you want the truth, or do you just want me to tell you what I think you want to hear?"

"Just say . . . something. I don't know what I'm doing here, Adrienne. I suck at this stuff."

"Tell me something I don't know. At this point I'm kind of getting the sense that you want me to play the role of supportive friend, so I say tell him to go fuck himself and make him sorry for the humping and dumping."

I just looked at her.

"Just saying what you wanted to hear. But in all seriousness, I really don't know. I would tell you to just dump any guy that didn't want you around his friends, but I also don't really know the entire situation since someone doesn't really talk to me much anymore."

"Sorry."

"It's fine. You just need to get your head out of your ass and start talking a little bit more. All I can say is just talk to him and figure out where you guys stand. There's no need in either of you wasting your time."

"Why are you always right?" I took in a deep breath. "Hey, do you want to just go do it for me?"

"Don't tempt me. You just have to rip off the bandage and stop being a little punk. You'll never know if you don't try."

"That's deep," I laughed.

"You can thank all the fortune cookies I've had over the years."

"Regardless, thank you once again. I'll talk to him and hopefully figure everything out." I stood up and stretched out the kink in my neck. "I'm gonna hit the sack."

"G'night."

"Night," I said, disappearing down the hall.

chapter **seventeen**

Things had been a little strange between Henry and I at the office since the conference. No, strange doesn't really seem like an adequate enough word for the situation. Weird? Awkward? Uncomfortable? Whatever it was, I didn't enjoy feeling like I was walking on eggshells.

I sat at my desk watching Henry run back and forth doing every demeaning task possible. Running for coffee at least five times a day, taking Cordelia's little ankle biter to the pet groomers, or leaving to grab lunch for people who were too cheap to use Uber Eats or DoorDash.

Henry stopped at my desk and leaned into it for support. "Oh, God. Is it always this exhausting doing everyone's dirty work?"

I suppressed a laugh. "Yes. It's really just their form of hazing or whatever. Give it a couple of months and they'll lay off. I went through it. I'm sure Kara and Theo went through it. We all had to deal with it at one time or another."

"Do they still pile everything up on you?" he asked.

"Kind of. I was the coffee bitch for a while, but then you came along. So, I guess that makes *you* the coffee bitch now."

"Oh, you're so funny." He crouched down and rested his head on the top of the desk and closed his eyes. I had never noticed before just how long his eyelashes were. They were enough to make any woman jealous. Hell, they kind of made me jealous.

He had this sort of perfection about him that I couldn't help but like. And I know I said that about Bennett, who was basically the perfect specimen in the looks department, but it was different with Henry.

Bennett was captivating and alluring, and you couldn't help but want to always have your hands on him. It was exciting. But with Henry, things just felt real. He made me feel comfortable and at home. In the past I'd never really found myself being attracted to the boy next door or even wondering what it would be like to be with someone like that. He was a complete dork, and for some reason I liked that for once.

I still owed it to myself and to Bennett to give things a solid shot though. Maybe I really was just overreacting about everything.

Henry opened his eyes and smiled up at me.

"Oh, I wanted to think you again for taking care of my head the other night."

"No problem," he replied.

"And about what almost happened before, you know, Theo called—"

He lifted his head up and looked me in the eye. "Oh, yeah. That was—nothing—right? Just a 'in the heat of the moment' thing."

"Totally," I stammered. "Stress levels were high, and people do crazy things when they're stressed."

"Besides, you have a boyfriend or whatever."

"Uh, yeah, I guess if that's what you want to call it."

"Don't sweat it. I won't tell."

"So, we're cool?"

"Totally." He smiled and jumped back up to his feet. "Alright, well I should probably get busy. Maya's got me reading through the slush pile to find anything worth her time."

"Have fun with that. Majority of the ones I've read have all been done by middle-aged suburban moms thinking they've written the next *Fifty Shades*."

"Fantastic. I'll see you later, bud."

Henry strode off to his desk on the other side of the room.

Bud? That's like something you'd say to your twelve-year-old cousin.

Maybe it really was just nothing to him.

chapter **eighteen**

Why was self-torture something I found enjoyable?

I hated the entire editing process. The long, grueling process of cutting out everything I was once so attached to just so it could all make plausible sense. But at the same time, I loved it. I loved how it all started coming together and turning into something enjoyable for others.

It was nuts.

I was nuts.

"So stupid," I said to myself while inking yet another red note onto the page.

Adrienne's head popped out from behind the fridge door. "What's stupid?"

"Just this entire chapter. I swear I must have been drunk when I was writing it."

"See, now that's impossible because you're a stick in the mud and I can't ever get you to actually drink anything."

"Getting drunk is overrated. Why would I want to put myself through the hangover the next morning? I can avoid it all together by just enjoying a glass of ice water."

She snorted from behind. "You're so lame."

"Better lame than hunched over a toilet and crying at three in the morning."

She pulled herself up on the counter and reached for a bowl on the top shelf of the cabinet. "Hey, I have never—"

"Freshman year in the dorms. We all went to that frat party and you two came back totally wasted. I had to walk you guys across campus and make sure you didn't get hit by a car."

"Okay, that was another time. I'm more mature now."

"What about our first night here when—"

Adrienne threw down a bag of cereal on the table. "I think that's enough walking down memory lane, mkay?"

I continued scribbling out more notes while she poured her breakfast.

Terrible. Awful. Decent? Pretty good. What the hell was I thinking? Kill with fire. This is so stupid. I'm so stupid.

I could hear Adrienne's crunching mixed with her attempt at breathing through a cold.

"Could you like not right now?"

"What? I'm eating."

"Could you eat a little quieter? I'm trying to focus here."

And the chewing got louder.

"Real mature."

The subtle pattering of feet came from down the hallway and I set down my pen. It was the first time I'd seen any real sign of life other than Adrienne in the apartment in days. Zoe made brief eye contact with me before grabbing a bowl out of the cabinet and taking a seat at the table, never

If I Fall

once saying a word. The cereal tinged against the bowl, triggering an eye twitch.

The sound of the cereal hitting the bowl, the milk jug scrapping against the tabletop, and their crunching I could tolerate if I tried hard enough. It was the sound of their spoons clanking against their teeth. It was worse than the editing.

"Sorry if we woke you up," I said.

"Whatever."

"I didn't hear you come in last night," Adrienne said.

Zoe took another bite of her cereal. "There was an accident, so I didn't get out until really late and I didn't want to wake you."

"Do you work again tonight?"

"No. I got the next two days off. The coordinator actually told me I'm not allowed to come back until Monday because I've worked too many hours."

Worked too many hours or drank too many bottles of tequila before work?

"At least you'll get some time to chill. Maybe we can all go see a movie or something this weekend? Like old times?" I said.

Nada.

"Or maybe we could have some people over tonight. Play some games and have some drinks."

"Wow, the snooze fest actually wants to drink." Adrienne said.

Zoe curled up in her seat. "Count me out. I'm just gonna sleep all day."

"Come on, it'll be fun," Adrienne said. "We can make margaritas. And you can invite that guy you went out with the other night. What was his name?"

"Actually, that guy didn't make the final cut. He was really weird and kind of a douche. But sure. Why not."

"Woo!" I looked down at my watch. "Oh, I need to go. I wanted to stop by Bennet's before work and see if we can talk."

"Good luck!"

Thirty minutes later I was standing in front of Bennett's apartment building. My heart was racing and I couldn't believe I was crazy enough to do what I was about to do.

An older woman walked out of the building and that was my chance. "Excuse me, could you hold that please? I forgot my key."

Either she believed me, or she just really didn't care. Either way it was a win-win situation for me. I rushed inside and into the elevator.

"Okay, you've got this. Just go in there and be confident. What's the worst that could happen?"

For starters, a lot could go wrong, but that's beside the point.

The elevator halted and the doors slid open. My chest pounded as I walked down the hall, my eyes never leaving his door. I stopped and stared at the letters 4E. Things were about to either go amazingly well, or terribly wrong. I knocked and heard feet shuffling toward the door.

"No turning back now," I whispered.

The door swung open and there he was. Standing in nothing but a pair of Calvin Klein briefs. Abs out.

"Wow."

He nudged the door closed a little. "Noah. Hey. What are you doing here?"

"I just had some time before I had to get to work and I thought I'd stop by and say hi."

"Oh, well, that's a nice surprise." He nudged the door just a little more.

"And I kind of wanted to talk. If that's cool with you, I mean."

What happened to going in with confidence?

I heard a thud from inside. "What was that?"

"Nothing," Bennett said.

"Is there someone else here right now?"

"What? No. I mean—"

Another pair of feet came shuffling down the hall. "Babe, do you want to take a shower before—oh, hi."

There was a stabbing pain in my chest, like someone jabbed a knife into my heart and just started twisting it. I knew I wasn't in love or anything and we weren't actually in a relationship, but I could have crawled under a rock and died. My cheeks burned.

"I see." I turned and looked at the guy. I thought I knew his face, but I couldn't place it.

"Noah, I can explain."

"Who's this, babe?"

"Pete, this is Noah. You know, the guy I was with the night we—"

"You were that awkward guy at the restaurant."

"Seriously? This guy?" I looked him up and down. I had to admit he looked a lot better without a shirt than I expected. And his abs were well defined for someone who looked like they weighed a hundred pounds when wet. Regardless, I wanted to punch him so bad. "This is the guy you're choosing?"

"I'm sorry. He slipped me his number after dinner that night and we started texting and really hit it off."

"So, your plan was to just lead me on all this time?"

"Lead you on? That's ridiculous. I was going to break things off, but you just got like super clingy and stuff. I didn't want to hurt you."

"Well, thanks for sparing my feelings and I hope you two have a wonderful life together." I headed back the way I came. I had to get out of there before I did something stupid.

"Noah, wait—would you just wait a sec. We can still be friends if you're into that."

I started laughing a little when I stepped onto the elevator. "I'd say go fuck yourself, but you seem to have that covered already! Go eat an eggplant."

chapter **nineteen**

My head was still reeling when I got to the studio. Everything was kind of moving at hyper speed and I couldn't believe I'd managed to make it on time. Or really at all.

I'd had half a mind to find the closest grocery store, buy several pints of Ben & Jerry's and just go back home and cry it out in the bathtub while listening to Demi Lovato's *Tell Me You Love Me* album on repeat. But I couldn't give him the satisfaction of having that much control over my emotions.

All of it made me want the win of the editor position that much more.

"Hi, I'm here for the Cordelia Collins interview," I said to the guard at the entrance.

The guard, who was quite large and sort of scary, looked me up and down. "And are you Cordelia Collins?"

"Uh . . . no. I'm Noah Carlisle. I'm an assistant at Hale Publishing."

He looked over the list of names on his clipboard. "Sorry, you're not on this list."

"You're joking, right? Just look again. You probably just missed it."

"I don't come to you and tell you how to do your job when you're grabbing your boss' coffee, so don't tell me how to do mine," he said.

"But—I need to get in there. Can't you just let me through? I can show you my badge and everything."

"Listen, kid. If I let you through because you have a fancy badge, then I'd have to let everyone through. Now beat it, there's a line forming."

"Thanks for literally nothing." I left the line and stumbled back to the sidewalk. I whipped my phone out and texted Theo. I knew if I talked to Jonathan about it I'd just wind up getting pissy and then join the ranks of the unemployed.

So not my day.

Dude. They won't let me in at the gate. WTF? Did someone forget to put my name on the list, I wrote.

It should be on there.

Eye roll emoji. *Yeah, well dick face at the door says I'm not on it and won't let me in. Can one of you like come out and get me?*

Give me a sec. We're talking to the producers right now. Be out in like 10 minutes.

Fine. I looked up just in time to see Maya's Lyft pulling up to the curb. *Actually, never mind. Maya just got here. She can get me in.*

She stepped out in her usual pant suit combo, followed by Kara, who I was sure would be loving fact that I wasn't even able to get in.

As I stood there, I tried to figure out exactly when everything started going to hell. Adrienne, Zoe, and I came to the city the day after Christmas, and I started working for Hale Publishing a week later.

Everything was great. I met with Kara and Theo. Zoe moved out like mid-July to live with her new boyfriend. Still, everything was okay. We didn't all plan to live together forever, so that was kind of inevitable. Somewhere between then and now everything started falling apart, and I just wished I could've gone back and fixed whatever it was that happened.

"Maya!" I shouted over all the noise.

Kara turned back and smiled.

"What are you doing out here?" Maya asked.

"Funny story. I think someone might've forgotten to put my name on the list."

"Oh, that must have been my bad. When I called, I thought I mentioned your name. I guess it just slipped my mind or something. Sorry," Kara said.

My gaze never left her. "It's cool."

Maya glanced down at her watch and motioned us along. She marched right up to the guard and stared him down. "Maya Reynolds, publisher at Hale Publishing. And these two are with me." She pointed back at me and Kara.

He didn't even bother looking at the list again. "Go on in, Ms. Reynolds."

We followed Maya inside and I gave the guard the stink eye on my way passed. For once I felt important. A high I could get used to, which also felt a little too dangerous for me.

I had never seen anything like it before. I'd been inside TV studios before for interviews with our smaller authors, but it was never anything as fancy as Leanne's. A mini Starbucks, a little bistro, gorgeous metallic interiors with large open spaces, and that was just the beginning. Maybe I really did choose the wrong profession.

We followed Maya backstage, where we found Jonathan and Theo chatting with some of the producers.

"Everything going smoothly?"

"It is now that you're here. Is Cordelia in hair and makeup?"

"I don't know. I just got here."

"She came here with you, right?" Jonathan asked.

"No—I thought she was with you."

"Um, hi . . . I would just like to make note here that I had absolutely nothing to do with any of this." Jonathan and Maya glared at me and I backed up before someone started swinging. "Wrong time. Wrong crowd. My bad."

I shouldn't have said it, but I couldn't help myself. For once it really wasn't my fault, and there was no way that Jonathan could say otherwise. I backed away until I eventually ran someone over and trampled all over their feet.

"Oh, I'm so sorry — Henry, I didn't realize you were here too."

"Yep. I just ran down to get some coffee." He looked at Jonathan and Maya who were at each other's throats again. "What's going on over there?"

"Oh, you know. Maya thought Cordelia was with Jonathan. Jonathan thought Cordelia was with Maya. And now there's like fifteen minutes till showtime and she's not here. The usual."

"Is that all?" Henry watched Maya and Jonathan passive aggressively bickering at each other some more. "Do they do that often?"

"Only when it comes to Cordelia. So, basically every day."

Henry and I strolled back to the group and watched pure hell unfold.

"Come on. Answer!" Maya yelled into her phone. "I warned her. You were all witnesses."

"Is it possible that she's just stuck in traffic and trying hard to get here?" Theo asked.

"Yeah, the day she isn't purposely screwing me over will be the day hell freezes over!" Maya screamed.

"Who screwed who over?" I heard from behind me.

Cordelia. Dressed up. Standing right behind us. Holding an iced coffee. And for the first time since I'd known her, seemingly sober.

"Where have you been?" Maya asked.

"Getting coffee. You can't expect me to put up with Leanne twice within a week and not have a pick me up."

Maya yanked Cordelia's coffee out of her grasp and pushed her in the direction of the cameras. "Whatever. Just get your ass out there, and if she brings up Saturday just say you got food poisoning from bad shrimp. Works every time."

We crowded around a monitor backstage and Cordelia joined Leanne on set. Watching Maya be so nervous about everything really made me wonder why anyone would want to do the job she does. For the first time, she showed real fear, which oddly made me respect her more as a person.

As great as it was seeing Maya embrace her badass woman persona, it was even better seeing her as a real human being; someone with real feelings that you could relate to.

Leanne's voice started booming from the monitor. "And welcome back. Our next guest is New York Times Best Selling author Cordelia Collins, responsible for novels like *A Beautiful Disaster*, *Playing with Love*, and most recently *The Getaway*. Thank you so much for being here today, Cordelia."

"Thank you for having me."

"I was so sorry that we didn't get to finish this last weekend."

"Me too. I'm so sorry I had to run out like that. I definitely don't see myself having shrimp again any time soon. Or any other type of sea food for that matter."

"But you're better now?"

"Absolutely. That care basket you sent was a miracle worker. Thank you so much."

She was hands down the master.

"She's good," Henry said.

I leaned in closer to his ear. "Oh, you have no idea. Also, my roommates and I are having some people over tonight for drinks and some games. You interested?"

"Sounds like fun. Will I be meeting this marvelous non-boyfriend of yours tonight?"

I'd almost forgotten about Bennett. "Uh, actually he won't be making it tonight."

"Oh, well maybe next time then."

"Things kind of ended this morning, so there won't be a next time."

The corners of his mouth turned up a little bit. "I'm sorry to hear about that. Probably for the best though, right?"

"Right."

Being out from under Bennett's thumb meant I could try things with Henry and not feel bad about it. At the same time, I didn't know if dating anyone was the wisest choice. Especially if that person was Henry. I had terrible luck with dating, and I didn't feel like ruining a potentially amazing friendship with him or making things more awkward at work than they already were.

"Alright, well that unfortunately is all the time we have for now. If you haven't already, go check out a copy of *The Getaway*. Thank you so much for joining us today, Cordelia. It was so much fun having you here."

"It really was. I promise I'll be back as soon as I can."

"You heard it here first, folks. Hopefully to promote another book that I can't put down."

"Could be."

Leanne smiled. "Join us tomorrow when Selena Gomez will be stopping by to talk about her next album and perform her latest single. Thank you all so much for joining us and have a great day. I'll see you tomorrow."

The outro music played and that was a wrap.

Cordelia actually managed to get through something with no sign of intoxication or vomiting.

It was kind of a miracle.

chapter **twenty**

"Wait, you caught him what?" Adrienne asked.

"In bed with the waiter from one of our dates. Okay, well I didn't actually *catch* them in bed, but I imagine they were in bed together when I knocked."

"Dude, that really sucks. I'm so sorry."

I pulled all the liquor bottles out of the cabinet and set them out on the table beside a pile of cards and board games. Looking down at all of it made me realize just how much we all looked like a bunch of alcoholics.

"When did we become drunks?" I asked.

"When we realized how terrible adult life is and we needed an escape."

"Sounds about right. I wonder what your students would think if they knew Miss Santiago was kind of a party animal sometimes."

"For starters I'd lose all power over them and they'd never take me seriously again. I'm pretty sure they think I'm a robot that the school just turns off at night and then reboots in the morning."

"Oh, so you're not a robot?"

Adrienne rolled her eyes and pulled the frozen pizzas out of the oven. Zoe came busting through the front door with a large brown box.

I jumped. "Whoa, did little Timmy fall down the well?"

Zoe tilted her head and vacantly stared. "What?"

"Never mind. What's in the box?"

She moved some of the bottles out of the way and slammed the box down on the table. She opened the flaps and pulled out a big speaker looking thing. "Isn't it beautiful?"

"What exactly are we looking at here?" Adrienne asked.

"It's a karaoke machine for tonight. Duh."

Zoe set it down next to the TV and strutted back into the kitchen.

"You've got to be kidding me," I said. "No way I'm doing that. I'd have to be totally wasted for that."

Zoe grabbed the bottle of UV Red from the table and waved it around in front of me. "Well get started. People will be here any minute."

Adrienne grabbed the bottle and poured some of it, along with some Sprite, into an empty cup. "Speaking of people, who all is coming? All the other teachers at school are kind of lame and didn't want to come."

Right. *All* the other teachers were lame. I could think of one who might've come had he been invited.

"I couldn't really find anyone to invite. Everyone else had to work the late shift so they won't be able to come," Zoe said.

"I invited Theo from work. And Henry." My stomach lurched when I said his name.

"Who's Henry?" Adrienne asked.

"Uh—just this new guy in the office."

"Okay, and? I need details. Your face totally just lit up when you said his name."

I started blushing and turned my back to them, trying to hide my reddened cheeks from them. Just saying Henry's name got me all giddy like I was a little high schooler with a crush again. It definitely didn't feel like any sort of crush I'd ever had though.

"Whoa, first of all, what happened to Benji or Barry or whatever his name was?" Zoe asked.

"It was Bennett. To make a long story short, he's an ass and all guys are asses."

"You're preaching to the choir, sister."

Adrienne chugged the rest of her drink and put her glass on the table. She pulled out a chair and then yanked me down into the seat next to her. Zoe picked up the box and set it down on the floor.

"I still need details. Who is he, does he have a criminal record, and most importantly—what team does he bat for?"

"He's the new assistant in the office. He took over for Theo after he was promoted to editor. We started hanging out during the convention last weekend."

"Go on," Zoe said.

"Well, after he helped me clean up the cut on my head again, there was kind of a—moment—if that's what you want to call it.

"What kind of a moment?" Adrienne asked.

"We kind of almost kissed, but the moment was over in like a second. It probably won't ever happen again. It was just a one-time deal."

There was a light tapping on the door. The little butterflies in my stomach were doing gymnastics.

Adrienne smiled. "Well, it looks like we'll find out tonight."

I hopped up and opened the front door. "Theo. Henry. You made it. And—"

Seriously?

"Kara, you came too . . . I mean, made it too. Yay. Come in." I stood aside and they all filed into the kitchen, which was feeling extremely tight with six people. "Well, you guys know each other," I said, pointing at Adrienne, Zoe, Kara, and Theo. "Henry, these are my roommates Adrienne Santiago and Zoe White."

"Nice to meet you," Henry said.

"So, you work at the publishing house with these three weirdos, huh?" Adrienne asked.

"Yup. Just started a little while ago. Unofficial title is coffee bitch, according to Noah at least."

"Hmm. And I bet you guys are always super busy. Late nights together in the office probably. All alone," Zoe said.

"Okay! Why don't you guys take your coats off and we'll put them up for you. There are some snacks in the living room. You guys can help yourselves." I smiled as they all took their coats off and hung them over a chair before heading into the living room to dig in. "Really? Those are the first things you say to him?"

"What? We're just curious. It's not like you tell us anything anymore," Zoe said.

"Well if anyone would know about secrets, it's you." I shoved some liquor bottles into the box the karaoke machine came in, along with some plastic cups and a couple things of soda and carried them into the living room. I dropped the box on the floor next to the couch and started pulling out some of the bottles.

Kara and Theo's hands were interlocked.

"When did this happen?"

"When did what happen?" Theo asked.

"You two being all lovey dovey."

"It's been a couple weeks. But, let's be real . . . it's been a long time coming. Did Kara not tell you?"

"Nope, I can't say that she did."

"Oh, it must have just slipped my mind. Sorry."

Right. The one thing that everyone's been waiting for finally happened, and it just slipped your mind. Seems logical.

We were all tipsy by 9 p.m. and decided to play a game of Cards Against Humanity.

"Come on, you have to pick a winner. You can't choose both," Adrienne said.

I looked down at my black card, which read *What gets better with age?* "I don't know. Why are you guys so good at this game?"

"Hurry up and choose!"

"Ugh. Okay. Robert Downey Jr. or Harry Potter erotica. Both good choices, but I think I'm gonna have to go with Robert. That man ages like a fine wine."

Zoe threw up her hands. "Yas! I win!" She took another swig from her glass. "And I believe that means I have five black cards now, which means I am victorious!"

"On second thought, I think I'm gonna go with Harry Potter erotica."

"Nope! You said it! You can't go back on it just because you're a sore loser."

Theo started piling all of the cards back into the box and Kara poured herself another glass of Cola and Captain Morgan, the drink I vowed to never let touch my lips again after the night Zoe moved back in.

"Z, why don't you go pick out another game," Adrienne said.

"Ooh, or we can start karaoke now. Noah's up first!"

"I'm gonna have to pass on this one."

"Come on. Do a duet with me! Like old times!"

"I'm not drunk enough for that, Zo," I said.

"Well then drink some more and get your butt up here."

Adrienne stood up and took the mic out of Zoe's hand. "Maybe we should just do something else." She leaned in closer and was barely audible enough for me to hear the rest. "And maybe you should slow down a little bit?"

"No way. I'm just getting started. But fine. If everyone is too chicken to sing, then why don't we just play a little game of truth or dare."

"How about no. We're not fourteen years old."

"Actually, that could be kind of fun," Adrienne said.

They were agreeing on truth or dare at the age of twenty-three? When drunk Adrienne and Zoe could agree on something like that, nothing good ever came out of it.

"I never got to play truth or dare, so I'm totally in," Kara said.

"Sure, I'll play," Henry said.

Zoe grinned at me. "Majority rules, so now we have to play."

Fantastic. No way that could get weird.

Adrienne and Zoe curled up together on the loveseat again and smiled at the rest of us.

"I'll go first," Zoe said. "And I choose truth. Someone ask me a question."

"Sure." Theo nibbled on his lower lip while he tried to think of a question. "Okay what is the most embarrassing thing to ever happen to you in public?"

"Oh, God. I remember this one time in college I was so over this class I was taking and my professor was a total jerk. I had to submit a final paper and I didn't realize until after he emailed me back that I forgot to change the name of the paper from Eff This Class, it's so Stupid and I Hate All of It before I turned it in. I also forgot to change his name back from Professor Shithead."

"I did that once. The professor was also my uncle," Theo said.

"You win. Hands down. That's rough." Zoe poured another glass for herself. "Adrienne, you're next. Truth or dare?"

"Truth."

"Who is the sexiest person here?"

"Oh, you know it's you, honey," Adrienne laughed.

"I knew it. See, painless wasn't it?" Zoe stared me down. "I believe that means you're up next on the Price is Right, Noah."

I could only imagine the type of shit Zoe would try to make me do. The last time we played truth or dare we were all living in the dorms and I wound up having to run down the hall in nothing but a towel. I was so happy it was too late for anyone in their right mind to be awake.

"Fine. Truth."

"Ooh, unfortunately since Adrienne and I both chose truth, you have to choose dare."

"No way. That's totally not a real rule."

"Oh, but it is," Theo said. "You've got to choose dare, dude."

Was everyone against me? I threw my head back and chugged the rest of my vodka lemonade before pouring myself another glass. If Zoe was giving the dare, I'd need it.

"Fine. Give me a dare."

"That's the spirit!" Adrienne said.

"Let me just think for a minute." Zoe and Adrienne exchanged glances and grinned from ear to ear. "Noah. I dare you to—" Zoe paused and her eyes shot back and forth between Henry and I, "give our new friend Henry here a little kiss."

I understood Adrienne and Zoe and their habit of interfering in other people's lives, but bringing Henry into the mix was not cool. Especially considering I'd just been chewed up and spit out by Bennett less than twenty-four hours earlier.

I looked at Henry, who seemed just as lost as I felt.

"Unless you're too chicken to do it. I'd hate for you to have to pay the penalty."

"You're bluffing."

"You want to put a bet on that?"

I really didn't. Zoe took her dares serious and I would've hated to find out what she had planned if I didn't do it.

"It's just fun, right?" Henry asked.

"Yeah, all in good fun. Be a good sport, you guys."

Evil.

Pure evil.

I took a deep breath, put my cup down on the coffee table, and stood up. It was really going to happen, and I couldn't believe I was doing it. How did I always get put into shady situations? I bent down in front of Henry's chair. "You sure?"

He smiled. "It's just a game."

I leaned in and planted my lips against his cheek. "There. Happy?" I said, turning to Zoe and Adrienne.

"Oh please. My abuela gets more action than that from her new boyfriend," Adrienne said. "A real kiss, or you have to pay the penalty."

"Ya'll are ridiculous."

Henry stood and looked me straight in the eye. It was crazy how beautiful his eyes were. I'd never seen that shade of golden brown before. The light reflected off them perfectly and I felt warmer just staring into them.

I caught my breath and felt his hand against my face. His other hand wrapped around the back of my neck and he pulled me down to meet him. I looked into his eyes for another second before I pulled him in closer and my lips met his. It was surprising how soft his lips were, and I only hoped mine weren't like sandpaper against his.

I was also becoming uncomfortably aware of the fact that even though I was thoroughly enjoying what was happening, everyone was probably still staring. I pulled away and fought a smile. His arms were still draped over the back of my neck.

"That's what I'm talking about!" Zoe shouted. "Who's next?"

The first time I kissed Bennett, I felt every emotion at once and I could actually feel my heart beating. My hands were sweaty, and my pulse was racing.

With Henry I felt completely at ease and totally comfortable. And I liked it.

I was in trouble.

chapter **twenty-one**

I woke to the sound of chiming from my MacBook across the room. Looking down at my phone screen on my bedside table, I focused in on the clock.

8am.

Who the hell was trying to FaceTime me at 8am on a Saturday?

I threw the covers off and trudged across the floor to my desk. My sister Brooke. Calling me at 8 a.m. on a Saturday. She was lucky she was like 900 miles away, because I could've slapped her.

I clicked the accept button and rubbed my eyes as her bright, smiling face popped up on the screen. "Brooke, what are you doing? It's way too early for this shit."

"Happy birthday!"

I cleared my throat. "What?"

"It's November 23. Don't tell me you forgot about your own birthday."

I looked down at my desk calendar. She was right. I did forget about my own birthday, which had never happened before. I used to love my birthday and made a big spectacle out of it the entire week leading up to the day. "Hm . . . I guess I did forget."

"You feeling okay, kid?"

"Me?" I asked, still avoiding her gaze. "Yeah, I'm just a little stressed out with work and stuff. It's no big deal."

"Are you sure? You know I'm always here if you need to talk. That didn't change just because you moved to the other side of the country. You're still my baby brother. Even if you are 24 years old now."

I nibbled at the inside of my cheek and let out a grunt. "Everything's fine."

Brooke's eyes narrowed. "You're totally lying to me right now. You've always been a terrible liar."

"What? How could you possibly know that?"

"I'm your sister. It's what I do. And you also start biting the inside of your cheek and fidgeting when you lie."

Betrayed by my own nervous habits.

"Fess up. Or I'm hopping in my car and taking a road trip."

"It's nothing. Honestly, there's just a lot going on right now with work and everything. I'm up for an editor position."

"That's so great, Noah! I'm so proud of you." Her eyes grew soft and her brows settled in a straight line. "But is that really what you want?"

"What do you mean? This is what I came here for."

"I know, but you also moved all the way there to write. Have you been doing any of that since you got there?"

"I know that's why I came here originally, but it's a rough game up here, Brooke. There are so many more talented writers than me not getting their big break. I think it's time that I just get my head out of the clouds and be realistic with what I have in front of me." I started running my fingertips along the edges of the desk. "I'm still writing, I'm just not going to hold my breath on a pipe dream."

She pursed her lips and her nostrils flared slightly. "I'm sorry. I just don't want you to give up on what you love like I did."

"I know. I'm not giving up, though. I'm just putting it on pause for now."

She stared at me for a moment like she was having trouble even recognizing me. Looking into the tiny window where my own face was, I had to admit I did look a little different than what I did before I moved to the city. I finally grew a stubble beard and truthfully my face was starting to look a little older from some of the stress, but I didn't think it was all that noticeable.

"You look . . . different," she said. "Have you been taking your medication?"

"I didn't really think I needed it anymore. I didn't see a reason for wasting money on it anymore."

"Noah—"

"I swear I'm fine. I can handle my anxiety a lot better than I used to. I haven't had any panic attacks or had any trips to the hospital or anything. Everything is good."

"Promise you'll get back on it if you feel like you need to."

"Yes. Fine. I promise that if it becomes a problem again, I will start taking it again."

"Sorry. I just worry about you."

"I know you do, and I appreciate it, but I'm a big boy." My phone vibrated against my hand. "It's Mom wishing me a happy birthday. How's she doing anyway? After everything? I haven't really talked to her much lately."

"About as good as can be expected. She has her rough days, but she's keeping herself busy with the girls. Have you heard from him at all?"

"Not a peep. Probably for the best though. He wasn't exactly father of the year or anything."

"I just hope he's okay."

"I'm sure he's fine," I said.

My phone vibrated again. This time it was a text from Henry.

Hey. A little birdie told me it was your birthday.

I held back a chuckle. *By little birdie, do you mean Facebook?*

That's another name for it, I guess.

Wrong app, I replied.

"Hello? Earth to Noah."

"Sorry. Just a birthday text from a friend."

"Oh? And would this friend happen to be a guy?"

"Yes, but he's just a friend. That's it."

"Mhm. I have to get off here, so I don't have time to beat it out of you, but I expect to hear about this soon."

"There's not much to hear, but okay. I'll talk to you later. You're still coming up for Christmas, right?"

"Wouldn't miss it. Love you."

"Love you, too. Bye!"

Brooke smiled one last time and then vanished from my screen.

You up for some breakfast? My treat for the birthday boy, Henry wrote.

Sure, why not. Just let me get ready really quick.

Good. I'm already outside your building.

chapter **twenty-two**

Henry and I strolled down 57th Street, and for the first time I actually started noticing couples up and down the streets, and not just the "traditional" couples either. It was a great change.

"Is it just me or is there a lot more romance in the city than normal?"

"Yeah, I noticed that too." Henry's hand brushed against mine.

I shoved my hands into my coat pockets. "Then again, it is cuffing season. So, I guess it's kind of to be expected."

Cuffing season? I'm so lame!

"So where are you taking me?"

"How would you feel if I said it's a surprise?" Henry asked.

"I would say you're making a huge mistake and that I'm about to get annoyed because I hate surprises."

"You getting annoyed would make things that much more fun. But fine, I'm taking you to this little bakery I found on my way to work one day. They have some bomb muffins and their coffee is amazing." He stopped in his tracks and I bumped into him.

"Ope."

"Did you just say 'ope'? I guess that really is a Midwest thing." He laughed and his eyes lit up. "Well, we're here. The Pastry Corner. I have to say the whole unveiling of where I was taking you went so much smoother in my head and didn't include either of us running into the other."

"It's cool."

He pulled at the handle and held the door open for me. I could smell the fresh pastries the second he opened the door, and I was in love. With the pastry smell, I mean. Not Henry. Although he had a nice smell that I was growing fond of too.

"I'll go order. What do you want?" he asked.

"Surprise me."

Henry raised his eyebrow and grinned. "But I thought you hated surprises."

"I only hate surprises when I don't know they're coming."

"I feel like you were the kid who organized his own surprise parties for his birthday."

"So what if I was?"

He brushed a stray hair off my forehead and smiled. "Go find us a seat and I'll order."

"Will do."

I found a little booth by the window at the front of the bakery overlooking the people as they passed by.

Looking back, I realized that the only places that Bennett ever took me were fancier places that were semi-dark all the time. And it was always in the far back corner of the restaurant. It was like he was ashamed to even be seen with me or acknowledge that he knew me. The only time we were ever around people, other than the party that I basically begged him to go to, was our breakfast picnic in Central Park. Even then, people weren't really paying any attention and it didn't last that long. It was all only on his time and I was too caught up to realize how stupid I was.

While I waited for Henry to finish ordering, I caught myself stalking Bennett's Instagram. And it was kind of sickening. He already had half a dozen posts cheesing it up next to Mr. Eggplant. One from a ferry ride across the Hudson. Another from a little #impromptuhike they went on together.

It was cute how he thought things would end any differently. Bennett wasn't capable of loving someone other than himself, and soon everything would come crashing down. It was all only a matter of time before his karma caught up with him.

The legs of the chair across from me screeched across the floor. Henry slid into the seat and set a coffee and white paper bag down in front of me. "Caramel iced coffee. It's my favorite."

I tore the wrapper off the end of the straw and stabbed into my drink lid. "That's good."

"Might be even better than Starbucks."

"Aye, watch your mouth. Do not mess with my Starbucks. I'd say it's a close second."

"Fine, I can live with that." Henry opened the paper bag and pulled out a couple of bacon, egg, and cheese croissants. "And you can't go wrong with a classic."

"Excellent choice." I peeled back the wrapper from my sandwich and took a bite. "Okay, that's amazing."

"Right? Everything here is made from scratch."

"I should start coming here more often."

"I'm down any time you are." He traced the lines of my palm with his finger and I pulled away yet again. He slid his hands back over to his side of the table and turned his attention to the window.

I was letting my own fear and insecurity ruin something potentially awesome as I usually did. I was afraid it was coming off like I didn't like him. "I'm sorry. It's just kind of a habit. I guess I'm still used to close minded Midwestern people and their homophobia."

"I get it. I've been here so long that I think I just kind of forget what it's like back home."

"I just need some time to get used to it," I replied.

"Totally. And if it helps anything, the owner of this place and his husband are totally accepting." Henry flashed another smile and took a sip of his coffee.

"So, tell me, how are you still single? Do you have an extra toe or something?"

"Yeah. I even have to get my shoes specially made." He laughed and it made my stomach flutter. "But for real, I just got out of a messed up relationship. An entire year of my life down the toilet," Henry said.

"I'm sorry to hear that. What happened there? If you don't mind me asking."

"We just turned out to not have that much in common in the end. I wanted to take the next serious step in our relationship, and he wanted to sleep with every guy on the Upper East Side."

Geesh. And there I was feeling bad about my situation.

"It's okay though," he continued, "it's better I find out now than another five years down the road."

"Still, that really sucks. I'm sorry."

"Everything happens for a reason, right?"

"Honestly, I used to believe that, but given recent events in life I don't know if I do anymore," I said.

He reached for my hand again and I resisted the urge to pull away.

"A year long relationship blew up in your face, and you're still so positive. How?"

"I don't know. I guess I just haven't been completely destroyed by the world yet. Give it time though, I'm sure it'll happen sooner or later."

I finished off my sandwich and took another sip of my coffee. I started out my day feeling really crappy about everything that went down with Bennett, and even though it was my birthday, I felt the need to do everything I could to cheer Henry up and give him the decent day he deserved. "Hurry up and finish your breakfast. There's some place I want to take you."

"Where?"

"It's a surprise."

"I guess I had that one coming," he said.

"Yes. Yes, you did."

He finished scarfing down his food and we drained the rest of our iced coffees. I loved me some ice coffee, but I wasn't about to carry that cold cup in 30-degree weather.

I grabbed him by the arm and whisked him out the door and back out onto the sidewalk. We dodged through the crowds and risked our lives cutting through traffic, stopping in front of the publishing house building.

"You wanted to bring me to work? You really couldn't think of anywhere else?"

"Patience is a virtue, Henry."

"And it's Saturday and no one's here."

"Rest assured there is always someone here." I pushed through the revolving doors and led him to the elevators. "The publishing world doesn't take a day off."

We took the elevator as high as it would go, and then I led him into the stairwell and up another four flights.

He paused for a moment to catch his breath. "If I'd known we were doing intense cardio today I never would've gotten out of bed."

"You good?"

"Yeah. Let's keep going."

"Don't worry, we're almost there." We pushed up the last flight of stairs and came to a long hallway. "When I first started here I kind of did a little bit of exploring. Eventually I found this place and it became one of my favorite places to eat on my lunch breaks over the summer. Once the weather started getting cold again, I stopped coming up here." The door creaked as I pushed it open and we walked outside. "It's not perfect, and it looks way better when the sun is setting, but it's still nice to look at."

His eyes lit up as he saw the city's skyline up close. The blaring of car horns and sound of construction below were barely audible. It was really the only place to go for a little peace and quiet. The air whistled around the buildings and blew through the thin layer of our coats. Henry shivered but was still unable to tear his eyes away from the sky.

"It's much nicer in the summer when it isn't so cold."

"It's great. It's the only part of the city I've seen that looks anywhere close to how the movies depict it," Henry said.

I zipped my coat up further and stuffed my hands into my pocket to try and warm them up. Henry turned back toward me, the sun highlighting the golden specs in his eyes.

"Thank you," he said.

"For what?"

"For sharing this with me. I know it was kind of your own little slice of heaven away from everything going on down there, so it means a lot that you'd open it up to me."

"What are friends for?"

He got closer and pulled me in tighter. His body heat was almost enough to help warm me up, but I got the sense I was more his heater than he was mine. He pulled my head down so my face was closer to his and I could feel his breath.

"Ooh. Coffee breath."

He pulled away. "Sorry!"

"It's fine." I pulled my hands out of my coat pockets and wrapped my arms around him. I slipped my hand under his chin and lifted his head up. It was our second kiss, but it still felt like the first, partially because the first time was under such forced circumstances. I pulled away and rested my forehead on his.

"I like you," he said.

"I like you too."

And that was what scared me the most.

chapter **twenty-three**

I found myself still dangerously floating on air Monday morning after spending most of my birthday with Henry.

It blew my mind that I was even capable of being so comfortable with a person after all the jerks I wound up dating in college, not to mention after Bennett. I was still trying to figure out how to let myself enjoy it.

I sat in the back of my Lyft realizing I'd made a huge mistake in not leaving sooner to avoid the morning traffic rush. It was way too damn cold to even think about walking. I had a love-hate relationship with the city. It was great being surrounded by opportunity all the time, but the sitting and waiting part was torture.

I rested my head against the window and pulled out my phone. There were only three days until Thanksgiving, and it would be the first one I'd spend without my family around. It was also the first I'd likely be alone. Adrienne had plans to go home and see her family, and since Zoe was living with us again in such close quarters, I imagined her family would have decided to fly her back home instead of coming to the city as planned.

I scrolled through my contacts to Adrienne's name and started typing out a new message.

Hey, what day are you and Z flying back home for Thanksgiving?

I'm not anymore, she replied. *My parents decided they wanted to come here for Christmas instead. And I think Z said something about not wanting to fly home twice within just a few weeks.*

I felt bad that they didn't get to go home and see their families either, but I was also kind of excited that I didn't have to spend it alone after all. Even if Adrienne and Zoe were still acting weird as hell and keeping secrets from me. At least I'd still have company.

I'm sorry. Frowny face. *Since ya'll are staying, maybe we can have our own little Thanksgiving, but maybe on Wednesday instead. We can invite some people over like we did for game night. Everyone can bring a dish.*

Sounds like fun.

You can bring anyone you want. Anyone at all. The more the merrier.

Was that a little too obvious?

K. I'll keep that in mind. Class is about to start, so ttyl.

Bye. Don't kill anyone.

I didn't know how she did it. One second with those high schoolers and I would have come out swinging.

We pulled up outside the publishing house and I tried to remember what it was like when I stood outside that beautiful building for the first time. Barely a year out of college, still mostly doe-eyed and hopeful for what my future would bring in the publishing world.

Now all I could feel was a sickening sense of regret and the longing to take a really long vacation somewhere tropical. It was difficult to love what I did when my entire job consisted of me doing everyone else's work they didn't want to do.

I forced my way into the building, despite my crushing desire to be literally anywhere else, and grabbed an empty elevator. I stood in the corner and leaned against the handrails. My body grew a little heavier with every floor until I reached floor seven. I readjusted my messenger bag and stepped out for another exhilarating day of coffee grabbing, email writing, and filing.

I found a cup of iced coffee from The Pastry Corner and Henry waiting at my desk.

"I stopped for a cup and I thought you could use a Monday morning pick me up too."

"Isn't that sweet of you. Thank you." I sank down into my chair and took a huge gulp. "Is this how druggies feel when they get their fix?"

"Probably." He grins down at me. "How was the rest of your birthday?"

"It was decent. Adrienne made me dinner and Zoe disappeared again and came home smelling like vodka and desperation."

He looked at me funny.

"Zoe's going through this whole thing. It's a long story."

"Ah. If you ever need any help with that whole situation let me know. I have a little bit of experience."

"Oh, so you like to come home reeking of vodka and desperation too?"

That got a chuckle out of him. "No, I just mean I have experience from a friend who was going through a difficult time too."

"I will keep that in mind." My eyes darted up in the direction of Jonathan's office, and he was giving me the stink eye. "I should probably get to work before Jonathan strangles me."

He peeked behind his shoulder. "That's probably a good idea. I'll talk to you later."

"Henry, wait. We were thinking about having like a Friendsgiving or whatever on Wednesday night since none of us are going home this year. Did you maybe want to come?"

"Sounds like fun and it gives me a reason to make my homemade stuffing." He leaned in closer so only I could hear. "And maybe we'll play another game of truth or dare."

It took everything in me not to kiss him then and there. "Sounds good. And if you see Theo can you invite him too?"

"Sure thing."

As Henry walked away, Kara stepped out of the elevator holding her Starbucks coffee and planted herself in front of her computer. It was beginning to feel like Serena and Blair level frenemy status.

"Morning, Kara."

She stared at me from the corner of her eye and silently returned to whatever was on her screen.

"How was your weekend?" I asked.

"Fine."

One word was still better than no word at all. It was a win in my book.

"Do you have any plans for Thanksgiving?" I asked.

She stopped typing and looked up at me. "Look, I appreciate that you're trying to converse and be social or whatever, but I have a lot of work to do. Think we can do this whole chit chat thing later?"

"Yeah. Sorry."

The door to Jonathan's office squeaked open and he stepped out. He approached my desk, and I knew I'd be regretting that I didn't call in sick just by the look on his face.

"Carlisle, do me a favor and call maintenance. Someone needs to look at that door."

I picked up the phone and started dialing the number.

"Not yet, Carlisle. I'm not finished." He took a sip from his coffee cup.

We were all beginning to look like drug addicts with the amount of coffee we drank on a daily basis.

"Lynch, this applies to you too, so pay attention. As it appears that neither of you is capable of convincing Cordelia on your own, Maya would like the both of you to try your luck and take Cordelia out for lunch. Anywhere she wants to go. You can take the company credit card."

"Both as in . . . together?" I asked.

"Yes. Both as in together. Do you not hear me when I'm speaking?" He rolled his eyes and headed back toward his office. The door squeaked again and he stopped. "Well don't just sit there. Get someone up here to fix this door. Now. And then when you're done get me on the phone with Christine from our office in London."

Kara tapped the table with her wrapped silverware. "Look, I'm not hating or anything. All I'm saying is that she could at least show up on time for a lunch that was being provided to her totally free of charge."

I checked my watch. 12:23pm. It would've been one thing to make plans with someone to grab lunch, and then they cancelled before you got to the restaurant, but it was another thing to just not show up. I didn't even want to be there. I didn't exactly have anything better to do, but I could've found something a little more enjoyable. Perhaps having all my eyelashes plucked out one by one.

"I'm sure she has a reasonable explanation."

Why was I defending her?

"Really? This is coming from the guy who nicknamed her the dragon lady?"

"I've grown since then."

"That was four months ago, dude."

"Okay, fine. I haven't always been the nicest, but it doesn't mean she necessarily deserves any of it. We don't know her personal life."

She squinted her eyes and dropped her silverware on the table. "Don't tell me that you're actually starting to like her as a person."

"I didn't say that."

"Don't get too attached. She's only one screw up away from being dropped hard on her prissy little ass."

"Oh, come on. We all know that was just a scare tactic so she wouldn't drink before the makeup interview."

Kara glanced behind her shoulder and at the front entrance of the restaurant. She leaned in closer to me. "I'm not even supposed to be saying this, but the company wasn't doing so well for a while. Maya had to go out and find people that were willing to invest in what a lot of people are calling a dying field. Everything is digital now and not many people are using print anymore."

"How bad are we talking here?"

"We wouldn't have made it to the new year. Why do you think Maya's been out of the office so much? She's been trying to track people down and beg them to invest. The people who finally did are no strangers to Cordelia's reputation, and her running out on that interview was the cherry on top for them. If she puts another toe out of line, then it's either drop her or they drop us."

"Can they actually do that?"

"They're paying for majority of our expenses now. They can do whatever they want, whenever they want."

It was ridiculous. Surely Maya wouldn't have allowed that to happen. They may have had their differences, but they practically rebuilt Hale Publishing together after the last publisher left the company to die.

I looked up and saw a waiter escorting Cordelia to our table. She looked like she hadn't slept in days. She had her trademark large black sunglasses covering her eyes, but I could only imagine what they looked like.

Kara kicked my leg under the table.

"Ouch!"

"Not a word."

The waiter pulled out Cordelia's chair for her and she sat. Rummaging through her bag, she pulled out a twenty-dollar bill and handed it to the waiter. "My usual please, Daniel."

He nodded and walked off.

How great it must've been to be able to walk into a room like that and just have complete power over everything. It's true when they say that money is power.

"You can close your mouths now. I think you're both drooling just a little."

She took off her sunglasses and it wasn't what I was expecting. I was imagining blood shot eyes, wincing due to pain from a hangover headache, and anything else that would point toward her drinking all night and all morning.

Instead all I found were dark circles, puffiness, and redness, like she'd just finished crying.

I couldn't tell if Kara noticed or not. If she did, then she sure didn't care enough to even pretend to be concerned.

The waiter came back holding a glass of champagne and set it down in front of Cordelia.

"You're late," Kara said.

"Someone's vigilant. Were you wanting a gold star now?"

Damn.

"What? No, I just—"

"Let me guess. Born and raised in Upstate New York, went on family vacations every summer until daddy dearest eventually got tired of mommy's excessive drinking, which she did purely to forget his countless affairs. You went to all the best private schools and eventually decided to major in the humanities as a big middle finger to your father. Probably earned your degree from—let's say—Harvard or something like that, where you graduated at the top of your class. How am I doing here?"

Kara looked like she'd just been shot or something. I couldn't believe I was witnessing all of it firsthand. I had to say that after all the crap Kara started putting me through after becoming her competition, it was nice to hear someone put her in her place.

"I did not go to Harvard. I went to Colombia," Kara stammered.

"Oh, well goodie for you. You must be really special to get into a place like that."

"No, I've just worked really hard for what I've achieved."

Cordelia took a sip from her champagne flute and then placed her hands over Kara's. "Sweetie, when you've had mommy and daddy pay for everything–which, judging by the looks of your outfit that no assistant in their early 20's would ever be able to afford, was pretty recently—you haven't had any real sense of achievement. Take it from someone who knows. Money can buy you just about anything, but it can't buy you respect or a sense of accomplishment."

Something told me there was a lot more going on up there in her head than she was leading on.

"So, the next time you want to question my life choices and why I'm late, just remember that money doesn't make you any more special than anyone else in this world." Cordelia downed the rest of her champagne and held out her glass. Another waiter rushed up to refill it. "So, let's get down to business here. First thing's first. I'm aware of the fact that Jonathan talked you two into coming here to talk me into selling the film rights. Let me save you some time by saying it's not going to happen."

At least she always got straight to the point.

"Second, there's this charity event on Wednesday night that I've been roped into going to. I could use someone by my side for the evening to help me out. What do you say, Noah?"

"Wait. You want *me*?"

"Is that a yes?"

"Look, that sounds great, but Wednesday night just isn't great for me."

Cordelia's eyes narrowed. "You do realize what I'm offering you, correct? The opportunity to rub elbows with some of the biggest names in the business."

I really did feel terrible, especially considering those events usually brought in a lot of attention from celebrities from every platform, but Friendsgiving was my idea, so I couldn't just back out of it.

"I appreciate the offer. I really do. I have another commitment on Wednesday evening that I really can't back out of."

"I'll do it!" Kara interjected.

"Of course," I let slip. "I mean—of course Kara would be a great choice."

Cordelia set her drink down and looked me up and down with her famous pursed lips and vacant eyes. She switched her view back and forth between the two of us. "Fine. Since you insist on throwing away an opportunity like this, I suppose I could give miss Colombia here a shot. Maybe you can prove yourself useful."

"Totally."

"And if you say the word totally one more time, you're out on your ass. Got it? Your generation can be so annoying. I just want to slap every last one of you sometimes."

"To—I mean—got it. It will not happen again."

Another point for Kara. Shocker.

Cordelia smiled and picked up her menu. "Let's order, shall we? I say choose the most expensive thing on the menu. You'll probably never get this opportunity again."

chapter **twenty-four**

I peered down at the stack of pages sitting in front of me. The amount of red ink that lined the margins made it look like the crime scene for a murder investigation.

It was the third round of edits for my manuscript and I was finally starting to feel a little hopeful that maybe the end result wouldn't be a complete disaster. It was no Stephen King novel, but it also was no longer just a heaping pile of crap. The closer I got to the end, the more terrified I was to let anyone read it or to hand it over for judgement. That collection of words was my baby, and I dreaded having someone tell me it was just a bunch of garbage.

I was startled back to reality by a pounding coming from down the hall.

"Zoe! Hurry it up! People are gonna be here and I still need to do my hair!" Adrienne beat her fists against the door a few more times. "You've been in there for almost an hour!"

I hopped off my bed and stuck my head out the door. "Aye! Could you not right now? I'm trying to focus, and I can't with all the yelling!"

A tiny pair of feet went stomping through the living room and then down the hall, stopping at my room. "I love her, but I'm going to kill her." Adrienne said. She jumped up on the edge of my bed.

"I love the fact that you're too short to just sit on my bed."

"Well then maybe you should have a lower bed." She ran her fingers through the tangled mess that was her hair and fell back. "If she plans on staying here much longer, then we need a bigger place. I cannot share a bathroom with her anymore."

"That involves money, something that we don't have a whole lot of. We can barely afford this place as it is." I collapsed beside her.

"Ugh! I know, I just can't take this anymore. I feel like I'm suffocating."

"We still have like two hours until anyone gets here. And we all shared a bathroom just fine before Zoe moved out, so why are you so stressed out? Doctor Carlisle is here to listen."

Fun fact: I was a psychology major going for my doctorates before I decided to follow my own path and become an English Education major, which then just become English. That may or may not be the reason it took me an extra year to graduate.

She sat up and gazed at the wall. "I have a date coming tonight."

I shot up. "What? Who?"

"Okay, I'll tell you, but you have to promise not to freak out." She avoided eye contact.

"Oh, God. You're not about to tell me you were sleeping with Bennett too all this time, are you? My life has become too much like a season of *One Tree Hill* as it is."

She gave me a swift kick to the back of the leg. "Don't be ridiculous. I would never date Bennett or any other guy you've ever gone out with."

"Because you're such a good friend and you'd never do that to me?"

"And I've seen the guys you've gone out with and most of them are—eh." She started playing with a piece of string that was unravelling from my comforter. "So, it's a guy from work."

Yup, I gathered that much beforehand.

"And I think you two would really get along. He's super cute and funny and really sweet. Did I mention he's really cute?"

"Name?"

"Tyler Willis—"

I had to think for a minute. "Willis . . . why does that name sound so familiar?"

"He may or may not be my boss . . ."

Didn't see that one coming. "I'm sorry, I think I might've misheard you. Did you just say you're sleeping with your boss?"

"I never said those words specifically . . . but in a nutshell—yes."

I slid off the mattress and started pacing back and forth while I tried to figure out how to form a coherent sentence that didn't make me sound like a complete ass. I stopped and opened my mouth before sitting down again. "Adrienne, you—do you realize how dangerous everything you just told me can be if the wrong person figures things out?"

"I know that. And we both know that this comes with some major consequences if it doesn't go well. We're careful about everything though."

"You can be as careful as you want, but eventually someone is going to figure it out. A stare that lingers too long. Spending too much time together. Getting caught outside of school on a date. One wrong move and everything could blow up in your face."

Adrienne catapulted herself up. "You think I don't already know all of this? I thought at least you would understand and give me a little bit of support."

I took her by the arm and pulled her in for a hug. "I'm sorry. If you're happy, then I'm happy. I just don't want you to wind up getting hurt."

"I know, but I'm a big girl and perfectly capable of handling this. I've been handling it since I got hired back in April."

"April? Are you kidding me? It's been going on since April?"

She pulled me in closer and tried patting my head, which turned into her practically slapping me in the face due to the insane height difference. "Shh. It's okay. We don't need to focus on that. What's important is that I'm telling you now."

"But—"

"Shh." She pulled away and walked toward the door. "I'm gonna go pull her out by her hair now. Dressed or not. Turkey should be done in like a little over an hour."

My phone chimed from the tangled disaster of blankets on my bed. I dove in and fished it out.

A new message from Brooke. *Please don't be mad at me.*

I started typing out my reply, but I was cut off by an incoming call from the Indiana area.

I swiped my finger across the green answer button. "Hello?"

There was breathing coming from the other line, and then a sound I never thought I'd hear again. "Hi, bud."

"Dad?"

"Yeah. It's been a while."

"Yeah, about nine or ten months to be exact."

"How've you been?"

What was I supposed to say to that? Life's been one huge shit show and I've almost reached my limits and I was barely holding onto my sanity by a thread? What was the proper etiquette for a guy who was barely there for your childhood and then just one day decided you weren't good enough for them to stick around anymore?

"Fine. Everything's been just fine."

"That's good. You still living in New York?"

"Yep."

"That's great. You like it up there?"

I leaned back against my headboard and started counting the ceiling tiles. "Look, not to be rude or anything right now, but I'm about to have people over so I don't really have a whole lot of time. Why did you call, exactly? I'm sure it wasn't for small talk."

"You're right. I didn't call for a bunch of small talk. I thought you deserved to know that you're gonna be a big brother. Amy doesn't like the idea of having a child born out of wed lock, so we're getting married next month, and I'd really like you to be there."

I caught my breath. "And you've told Brooke all of this?"

"She said she'd only go if you did."

"So, you really expect us to attend a wedding, after not talking to any of us for several months I might add, in which you're marrying a woman that you left our mother for not even a year ago, all for a kid that you're having with said woman?"

"I get how upsetting this might be for you, but you don't know the entire picture. Your mother and I weren't happy for quite a while. The last year of our marriage wasn't good for anyone involved. This is my second chance at a life."

"Second chance at a life?"

"I didn't mean it like that. I mean this is a second chance for all of us. I messed up big time, and I want to make it right."

"You're right. You do need a second chance. And I'd hate for your first chance at life to mess things up for you again."

"Noah, I—"

"Do me a favor and please don't call this number again. I hope you have a nice life and good luck on your wedding. Maybe try not to abandon this next kid, okay?" I felt a lump in my throat. "Goodbye, Dad."

My last few words came out broken before I pressed the end call button. I burrowed into my pile of blankets and began to understand why people turned to alcoholism to deal with their problems. It was a hell of a lot easier to deal with all the crap in your life when the emotions attached to all of it were numbed.

As I lay there, I remembered there was still half a bottle of wine siting on the top shelf of my closet from a night of drinking with Adrienne from a couple months before. And I still had almost two hours before anyone was supposed to be there, so it was the perfect time to finish it off.

chapter **twenty-five**

After I finished off the half bottle of wine hidden in my closet, I wasn't really feeling anything and figured a couple more glasses from the stash above the fridge wouldn't hurt while I waited for everyone to arrive.

The girls came into the kitchen while I was putting the finishing touches on my cheesecake bites for dessert. Zoe was wearing a purple blouse and a pair of black skinny jeans, while Adrienne pulled out all the stops with a little black dress that wasn't too revealing, but also not too prudish.

"Someone's trying to earn some extra credit tonight," I said.

"What?" Zoe asked.

"It's a long story," Adrienne answered.

"Well, it's not that long of a story. Our little angel here has a date for tonight."

"Ooh, girl. Get it! It's about time you got some."

"Her boss," I said.

"Oh, my — Adrienne! You realize this could go terribly wrong, right?"

"Boy, I know where you sleep," Adrienne said. "He's already given me this entire talk, so please just don't do anything to embarrass me tonight. Please?"

"Fine. I guess I'll go put away all the pictures from college," I said.

"Stop! You're terrible! And just for that I'm stealing one of these." She swiped one of the cheesecake bites from the tray and shoved it into her mouth.

"Hey! Those are for our guests. But I guess I had that coming." I filled up my wine glass again. "Anyone want any before I finish this puppy off?"

"Me!" they both shouted at once.

I reached into the cabinet and grabbed Zoe and Adrienne a wine glass each. I filled both halfway and then sucked the rest of the bottle dry.

"We need more wine," I said.

"Isn't there a bottle in your closet?"

"Nope. Drank that too."

"Wow. Are you feeling okay?" Adrienne asked.

"Totally. Why do you ask?"

"It's just that you don't usually drink anymore unless something's wrong. Anything you want to talk about?"

"Nope. Everything's great. I'm great. Life is just—what's the word?"

"Great?" Zoe asked.

"You know me so well."

I took another sip from my glass when Ariana's *bad idea* started blasting from my phone. I dug through the drawer next to the stove and pulled out a couple of oven mitts. If there was one thing from my childhood that I was fortunate for, it was that my mom was adamant on me learning how to do my own cooking so I wouldn't starve to death when I was one day living on my own.

I opened the oven door and pulled out the turkey and set it on top of the counter. I could practically feel my mouth watering as soon as I smelled it. "Not to brag or anything, but damn, I've done it again." I turned off the oven and pulled the mitts off my hands. "Okay, so we have the turkey, mashed potatoes are on the stove, Hawaiian roles in the cabinet, and cheesecake bites for dessert. Henry's bringing the stuffing and yams, I think. And then Theo made mac n cheese."

"I told Tyler to bring drinks and some plastic cups."

"Awesome. I believe that is everything. Our first Friendsgiving will start in t-minus—"

There was a knock on the door.

"—now I guess." I skipped across the kitchen and yanked the door open. "Howdy!"

Theo and Henry stood on the other side staring at me like I was on crack or something. In their defense, I could've been for all they know. I was acting like it. I pulled one of the containers from Henry's grasp and shuffled back to the counter.

"Someone seems happy," Henry said.

"Well, I'm almost an entire bottle of wine deep right now, so I sure hope so. Otherwise that's some lame ass wine." I pulled Henry in and planted several kisses all over his face.

"And before you ask, we're out of wine for the time being. But we still have a liquor store's worth of vodka up in the cabinet if anyone's interested," Adrienne said.

"Maybe later," Theo said.

"Probably a good call."

"So, is this like a thing now? The two of you, I mean," Zoe asked.

I exchanged glances with Henry. Neither one of us knew an answer to that question. We hadn't actually talked about that part yet.

I surveyed the kitchen, trying to think about what was missing. "Crap, I forgot the table extender thing."

Adrienne took another drink and placed her glass on the counter. "I'll get it. I think it's still in the hall closet?"

"Should be. Thank you."

Adrienne took off down the hall, her heels clacking against the floorboards. There was another knock on the door. My guests had already arrived and there was only one person left to join the party.

"Adrienne! Door!"

"Can you get it?" she shouted from down the hall. "And don't say anything stupid!"

She knew very well that I couldn't make a promise like that.

The door swung open and I froze. Talk about tall, dark, and handsome. His outfit was perfectly tailored for his body, showing off every curve of his biceps. And his eyes were something you could get lost in if you stared long enough. I could see why Adrienne was so tempted to break the rules with him.

"Hi, you must be Tyler."

"And you're . . . Noah?"

"That's me."

Oh my, God. He knew my name. And he said it in that voice. Why couldn't I ever find a hot English guy?

I invited him in and took the bags out of his hands. "And this is Zoe, Theo, and Henry."

"Nice to meet you all."

Adrienne came hobbling down the hallway. I forgot the table extender was almost half her body weight. Add heels to the equation and it wasn't a fun time for her.

Tyler jumped in and grabbed it out of her hands. "Hey, let me help you."

Adrienne smoothed out her dress and moved her hair back into place. "Thank you."

Zoe and I spread apart the leaflets of the table and Tyler shifted the middle extender into place. He made it look so effortless. It usually took me a solid two minutes to jam that thing in place and line it up just right.

"There we go," Tyler said.

"I guess that's it. Everyone grab a plate and dig in!"

A line quickly formed, starting at the turkey and ending with the homemade mac n cheese that Theo brought. I was planning on trying that later, although my lactose sensitivity wasn't going to enjoy it as much as I was.

I pulled Adrienne aside before I grabbed my plate. "Holy shit."

"I know, right? I think this one's a keeper."

"Better be careful, I might snatch him up if you don't want him."

"Oh, honey. Over my dead body."

"Note taken."

My phone rumbled against the coffee table. I may have been extremely buzzed, but I didn't think I would have been able to handle another conversation with my father if that was him again.

Good news: It wasn't him.

Bad news: It was Kara, rubbing my face in her win with a selfie of her at the charity ball with Cordelia and—Oprah? Just another reason for me to want to escape from everything.

I needed more wine.

Vodka sounded nice too.

"So how long have you three known each other?" Tyler asked.

"We all met in the dorms our first year at Illinois State. We've never really been apart since then," Zoe said.

"And I'm guessing you have a lot of stories to tell."

Adrienne nuzzled closer into the crevice of Tyler's arm. "Oh, you don't really want to hear any of those."

"Oh, but I really do."

I sipped a little more of my vodka lemonade. I could feel myself kind of phasing in and out of consciousness, but I was present enough to think about all the stories I wanted to share about Adrienne. If not for Tyler, then for the nostalgia of a much simpler time.

"Okay, I have one," I said. "It was senior year and a group of us decided to take a trip for spring break. Well, someone in the group decided to bring some weed and this one over here wanted to try it for the first time. After the first hit she coughed so hard she actually threw up everywhere. Like, full on projectile."

"Noah!" Adrienne yelled.

"Oh, sorry. I forgot your date was your boss. Did you guys know Adrienne was dating her boss? I don't want to get you sent to the principal's office or anything." I started laughing harder than I should have, especially considering she asked us to not embarrass her. It just came spewing out. "I guess you don't ever have to work very hard to get a raise or anything, am I right?" I took another swig of my vodka and slammed my empty cup down on the table. "Who wants more vodka?"

"Noah, do you think maybe you've had enough to drink tonight?" Zoe asked.

That got me started. I would've thought that knowing Henry was sitting across the table from me would have been enough to make me keep a little sanity, but by that point I was passed the point of caring about anything at all.

"Hmm, this is coming from the girl who hasn't been sober in like . . . weeks. I'm not even kidding. The release party for Cordelia? Drunk. During her shifts at the hospital? Drunk. Every night. Hey, maybe that's why your boyfriend left you."

If I could go back and time and punch myself in the face, I would not hesitate.

"Noah, lay off!" Adrienne screamed.

"Aye, you've been just as curious about her little secrets as I have. Speaking of which, I walked into the school one day to bring this one lunch and caught these two making out in her classroom like a couple of teenagers. Hope you got some extra credit!"

Henry grabbed my hand. "Noah, I think you've said enough."

"He's right. And I for one have done enough listening for tonight, "Adrienne said. She threw her napkin down on her plate and stood up. "Is it alright if Zoe and I stay with you tonight? I don't really feel all that comfortable here right now."

"Of course. Whatever you need. Just go get your things and I'll go wait outside for a car," Tyler said.

"Thank you." Adrienne grabbed Zoe and they fled to their room to pack a bag for the night.

Tyler waved goodbye to Theo and Henry, disappearing through the front door.

Theo grabbed his plate and set it in the sink. "Hey, so I think I'm just gonna call it a night. You two have a good one."

"Yeah, you too," Henry said.

Theo opened the front door and found a straggler in a black ballgown holding a bottle of champagne and hanging out in the doorway.

"Cordelia?"

"Hello, I was in the neighborhood and I thought I'd drop by. Does anyone happen to have a king size bed and some feather pillows I could borrow perhaps?"

"How did you even know we were here?" Theo asked.

"Well, I knew you were having a little dinner party, so I figured I'd stop by. I found this address in a file. This place is a fucking *dump*," she said in between her laughs.

"And where's Kara?"

"The hell if I know. Who wants to make me a drink?"

Theo turned and looked at me and Henry. I was too drunk to actually understand anything that was going on.

"You look tired. Would you like to sit down?"

"Oh, yes. Thank you so much." Cordelia flung her arm around Theo's shoulders and he half dragged, half carried her to the couch. "You're so sweet. And not bad on the eyes. You've always been one of my—one of my favorites. Where's my drink?"

Not long after, Cordelia was out like a light. Had I been more aware of what was happening, I might have been a little annoyed by the fact that she now knew where I lived and could come annoy me at any time of the day. Home was my only safe space.

Henry grabbed me by the hand. "Okay, I think it's time we got you to bed too, okay?"

"Okay, good sounds to me. Wait, no. That's not it. I mean, that's good sounding to me. Nope, that's not it either."

"It's fine. I get what you mean."

Henry wrapped my arm around the back of his neck, and he escorted my clumsy self down the hall and to my bed. I kicked off my shoes and stripped off my button up and skinny jeans.

"What was that out there? You were kind of being an asshole."

"Oh, come on. They know I'm just messing around. It's just a little fun." I sat at the edge of my bed and pulled him in by his belt loops. "Speaking of fun, what do you say you and I have a little bit of our own fun right now?"

"Stop. You need to sleep."

"Don't be such a stick in the mud. It's no big deal."

"Well it is to me, Noah. I don't want our first time to be like this."

"Again, who the hell cares. Let's just go already."

"And I said no, Noah! What part of that do you not understand right now? I'm not going to take advantage of someone like that. Especially—someone that I'm falling in love with. I wanted it to be special."

He pulled away from my grip and I leaned back.

"You're falling in love with me?"

"Well, I thought I was. At least until I saw what you did out there."

"Can we talk about it?"

"Maybe. Just not right now. Get some sleep and call me when you're done with whatever the hell this new attitude is."

Henry turned and walked away, closing the door behind him. I collapsed on my bed and stared up at the ceiling. My focus was going in and out, but even then, I knew that I majorly screwed everything up, and I didn't know if I would ever be able to fix it.

chapter **twenty-six**

I never understood why I would avoid getting drunk and say how stupid it was, just to turn around and drink more than what I assumed was humanly possible and complain about my decisions the following morning.

Drunk me and next day me were not on speaking terms anymore.

For a moment, I lay in bed gazing up at the ceiling and wondered why I had such a headache. Then it all came rushing back. Embarrassing my best friends in front of everyone, being a total ass hat, and being extremely weird and forceful with Henry.

And, worst of all, Henry telling me he was falling in love, but I somehow managed to destroy every sliver of that in one night. I was terrified that he would wind up breaking my heart and walking out like everyone else always did, but I was the one that messed things up.

I broke my own heart this time.

I jumped out of bed and threw on a pair of flannel bottoms and a t-shirt I picked off the floor. I flung the door open and rushed across the hall to Adrienne's room.

"Adrienne? Zoe?" No one. I raced down the hall and into the kitchen. "Anyone here?" I plopped down into one of the chairs.

The thing that I wanted to avoid the most actually happened. I was completely alone on Thanksgiving, and I had no one to blame but myself. I figured there was no sense in trying to call anyone and apologize. The chances of them actually answering were slim to none.

"You're really whiny, you know that?"

I stood up and slowly made my way into the living room. There I found Cordelia wrapped up in a blanket like a burrito, her hair in a puffy mess, makeup all over her face, and countless bobby pins scattered all over the coffee table.

"Uh . . . how did you—" And that's when I remembered she was kind of a stalker the night before. "Oh." I took a seat on the loveseat and just awkwardly sat there trying to figure out what to say next.

"Cute place you have here."

"I vaguely remember you using the word 'dump' to describe it last night."

"Well compared to my place it's a dump, but not bad considering the neighborhood, I suppose." She hid her face from the sun streaming in through the windows.

"No offense, but you look like you've died and come back to life."

Her voice was muffled through the cover. "Trust me, sweetheart. You don't look too great yourself." She ripped the blanket off her head and looked at me. "Be a doll and find my purse for me. I need to take something before my brain explodes."

"I have some Walgreen's brand pain medication if you wanted some of that."

"I grew immune to that baby stuff a long time ago. I need my purse. I think I dropped it by the front door last night."

I rolled my eyes and went searching. "So, did you just leave in the middle of the charity thing last night?"

"It was getting boring, though I'm not quite sure how I ended up here. This place isn't much better."

I found her purse hanging from the front closet door handle and carried it back into the living room. "And you just left Kara there?"

"From what I remember she was having fun. I'm sure she didn't even notice I was gone."

No, I was sure she probably noticed. If she didn't then Theo probably told her on his way out.

Cordelia took her purse and started digging through it like a mad woman. Why do women need such large purses? They spend majority of their time digging through them like they're looking through buried treasure anyway. A small bag would be way more convenient and easier to carry.

I heard a pill bottle hit the wood flooring and roll across to the other side of the room. "I'll get it."

"No. it's fine. You don't have to—"

I was already up chasing after it. "It's cool, I don't —" I glanced down at the label. Fentanyl. Why would she need those? "Cordelia, these pills are — Why do you have these?"

She sat up and glared at me. "I just get really bad migraines. It's the only thing that works for me anymore."

"I happen to know that these are a step above morphine, and I don't know any doctor who would prescribe them for migraines. And they have your name on them, so I know for a fact that you didn't just buy them off a random person. I have an aunt who got these for pain when she was diagnosed w —"

I sat down again and looked into her eyes. "Cordelia, why do you have these?"

I held them up in front of her face and her eyes darted back and forth between me and the bottle. She started squinting and rubbing her temples. I threw the bottle into her lap and got up to close the gap in the curtains.

"Fine, don't talk. But I'm sure Maya will love to find out that her star author is taking opioids. Maybe she can get it out of you."

"Oh my, God. You don't quit, do you? Sit down."

I took a seat again and waited patiently for an answer.

"I'm dying." She said it so nonchalantly. "I was told I have maybe a year to live, and that was almost six months ago."

"What? If this is some kind of joke, it's not funny, Cordelia."

"Oh, I wish it was a joke. Went in to try to figure out why my migraines were getting much worse, and several tests later, turns out I have a brain tumor."

I leaned back and sunk further into the cushions. "Well, it's curable, right? Lots of people beat cancer. They can do surgery or something."

"It's inoperable. Doctor called it a glioblastoma. They said they could try to do surgery, but there was a very high chance I'd wind up brain dead by the end of it. I'd much rather die with my dignity than be a vegetable for the rest of my life."

"Have you told anyone else? Like Maya, perhaps? Or your son?"

"I don't see why anyone else needs to know. It's none of their business. As for Owen, he made it very clear a long while ago that he doesn't want me in his life. It's better this way." She pulled a flask out of her purse and downed one of her pills.

"I don't really think you should be taking those with alcohol."

"What's it matter? I'm already dying." She took another swig and set the flask down beside her.

It all finally made some sense. All the drinking and the weird changes in attitude. She was always a little harsh, but she at least had the decency to not purposely pounce on people before her diagnosis.

"Still, I think you should maybe slow it down a little."

"Why?"

She needed to know. She deserved to know everything. The investors basically taking over the company, the position they were putting Maya in, and that her days at Hale Publishing were numbered if she didn't pull her act together.

"There's some things you need to know. The company was having some problems and so Maya had to get some people to help out and—"

"And they want to me get my shit together, or I'm out on the curb."

"You knew?"

She laughed. "Maya and I may not always get along, but we've been friends for years. She'd never let that happen without putting up a fight."

"If she knew about your tumor, then maybe—"

"I don't want to bother her or anyone else with the details. I don't want to be looked at as weak. I want to go out with some dignity and grace, knowing that I fought tooth and nail until the very end."

As hard as it was going to be keeping a secret like that, I had to respect how much strength Cordelia had, even during the roughest time in her life. That was the person that I looked up to, not the alcoholic mess that I saw every other day of the week.

"Do you want some tea or something?"

"How about a mimosa?" She smiled when she realized I was two seconds away from strangulation. "I'm kidding. Tea sounds nice."

I wandered into the kitchen and pulled a couple of glasses from the cabinet above the sink, after which I realized my head was still pounding, so I reached into the designated junk drawer and pulled out a bottle of off-brand ibuprofen.

I popped off the cap of the bottle and counted out four of the little tablets in my head. I pulled a pitcher of tea off the top shelf of the fridge and filled each glass about half full.

"Hey, do you want any lemon in your tea?" I popped the pain killers into my mouth and hoped they would start working soon. "Cordelia?" I picked up her glass and trekked back to the living room. "Where'd you go?" I followed the trail of her perfume down the hallway and into my room. "Hey, what are you doing in here?"

She turned toward me, and she was holding my manuscript in her hands.

"You don't want to read that."

"Did you write this?"

"Um—yeah. It's not really that great, though."

"This is really good."

I handed her the glass of tea and took a drink from mine. "You think so?"

"I mean, it could use some tweaking, but I think you've got something here." She flipped through more of the pages and chuckled.

"What?"

"Just this line you wrote. It's really funny." She laughed again and turned another page. "Is this what you want to do? Writing, I mean."

"Yeah, or at least I used to. I don't really know anymore."

She placed it on my desk, treating it like a newborn baby. "You really think it's good?"

"Yes. And believe that I wouldn't say so if I didn't believe that whole heartedly. Can I give you some advice? Writer to writer."

"Yes. That would be amazing."

"Don't waste your talent."

"That's easy for you to say. You're a world-wide phenomenon. The chances of me getting anyone else interested in this thing are practically one in a million. It's probably just best I stick with what I know."

"Which is working under Jonathan in a position that you very obviously hate? Makes sense. You know what they say. When the going gets tough, the tough hide behind a sad little man working for less than they deserve." She took a sip of her tea and set it down.

I followed her out into the hallway and to the front door.

She turned the knob and then looked one last time. "Call me when you're ready to stop cowering in fear and do something with that."

chapter **twenty-seven**

It had been a week since my entire life combusted. Henry was barely speaking to me, Theo avoided having to have any sort of non-work-related discussion with me, Adrienne was staying with Tyler and only came back when she needed more clothes, and Zoe was staying with a friend from work and wouldn't even speak to me anymore.

Everyone hated me, but I couldn't say I didn't deserve it. I would hate me too.

I sat at my desk, just watching the time tick on. Ten more minutes until I was free for the night. Not that I had anything to do afterward. The last few minutes of my shift, I turned to time travelling through my old Instagram posts, wishing I had Hermione's time turner so I could go back to a time when I didn't have to have everything figured out and my biggest problem was passing a math test. How did I make such a mess of things?

I heard Kara from her desk. "You out of here, Henry?"

I peered over my monitor, trying not to look creepy, but with the state of things, that wasn't really possible.

"Yes. You working late tonight?"

"Unfortunately."

"Well, don't work too hard. Have a good night," Henry said.

"You too."

I shut my computer down and snatched up my things to catch the elevator before I lost my chance for a ride alone with Henry. "Hold up!" I shouted. I shoved my foot in between the closing doors and stepped on.

He half smiled and took a step closer to the wall.

"It's been a while," I said.

"Yeah."

I twisted my body around to get a good look at him. I knew the odds of him wanting to talk were low, but I had to make things right sooner or later. "Do you maybe want to go grab some dinner somewhere?"

"I don't know, Noah. I think I just need to take some more time."

"Okay, no food. How about just coffee then? I'll pay for me and you'll pay for you. No hand holding or anything else. Not a date. Just talking. That's it."

He looked up at me. "Fine. One coffee."

We wound up at the little bakery that he took me to on our first date. Though, something told me that things wouldn't go as friendly as the first time around. We grabbed our coffees and found a table.

I just sat staring at the tabletop for the first few minutes while he played a game on his phone. "How was your Thanksgiving?"

"It was fine."

"That's good." The small talk was getting me nowhere. "I just really wanted to say I'm sorry about . . . well . . . all of it."

"Where did all of that even come from? I was totally confused and have no idea what to think."

Where to start? My estranged father tried to sneak back into my life, I was practically being stalked by a world famous writer, who also happened to be dying and I was the only one who knew, so no pressure there, my best friends were lying to me about basically every new detail of their lives, and my boss was an asshole for a reason I couldn't figure out. Oh, and I didn't even know if I actually wanted the job offer that was destroying one of my closest friendships.

"There's just a lot going on in my life right now. And I know that's no real excuse, but I'm really sorry."

"You're right. That isn't a real excuse. We all have stuff going on in our lives right now and we're all trying to figure things out, but that doesn't give you the right to act the way you did."

"I know. And I'm so sorry that you had to see all of that."

He rested his head on his hands and looked away from me.

"Did you mean what you said that night? That you're falling for me?"

"Maybe—I don't know. I guess I was falling for the version of you that I first met. But, after what I saw, I don't know which version of you is the *real* you anymore."

"I'm still the guy you met and watched videos with, Henry. That guy from the other night, that's not me. I swear."

He sipped his coffee and took a deep breath. "The last couple months of my last relationship weren't ideal. In between all the lying and the cheating, he turned into someone that I didn't really know anymore, and I guess now I'm just terrified of something like that happening again."

"And I totally understand where you're coming from. Until you, it was always kind of the same thing with guys. And I think that's kind of taken a toll on me. I think I just chickened out and tried to sabotage things before you came to your senses."

"Maybe we just jumped into this too fast," he said. "Maybe we just need to take a little more time to just be with ourselves and get to know each other a little more."

My heart was trying to leap out of my chest and throw itself through the window, but for once I needed to listen to what my head was telling me. "I don't want to say it, but you might be right."

"And then maybe—sometime down the road—if we both feel the time is right, we can try this whole thing again."

I took one last look into his beautiful golden-brown eyes and forced a smile onto my face. If I was going to agree to that, I couldn't allow myself to do anything that would risk catching stronger feelings.

"Friends for now?" He held out his hand.

I extended a hand and shook his. "Friends for now." I flashed a smile and let go of his hand. "I can play the long game."

Now I just had to figure out what you did with someone you've made out with and were now just friends with. Couldn't really be that difficult, right?

chapter **twenty-eight**

I shifted my line of vision between the stack of pages and the word document pulled up on my screen. I reached for my coffee and remembered I sucked the rest of it dry twenty minutes earlier. I kept reaching for it out of habit. I really wanted a coffee from The Pastry Corner, but I didn't feel right going there without Henry. Plus, a freak snowstorm hit the city and I didn't really feel like going that far from home for a cup of coffee and a place to write. So, Starbucks it was. Not that I was complaining.

"No, that's not right," I whispered to myself.

I studied the page in front of me trying to decipher a note I made for myself when it came time to typing out the last few details. I was always told my handwriting would improve with age. It actually got worse, which I didn't think was possible.

I squinted and turned the page in several different directions before I finally figured out I was looking at a C and not an E. I returned to the keyboard and finished typing out the last sentence of the page. I reached for my cup again. "Oh my gosh." I reeled my hand back in and used it to flip the page upside down on the rest of the stack. Glancing down, I took a moment to process that there weren't any more pages. I dialed in on the screen and realized I had just written the final edited line. "Oh my gosh. I did it. I really did it."

I picked up my phone and started typing out a celebratory text.

Adrienne! It's done! I finished it! I actually finished the—

My thumbs stopped and I remembered that she still wasn't speaking to me. The only person who was there from the conception of the story and was actively following it didn't even want anything to do with me.

I deleted the text and put my phone back down on the table. I flipped the stack back over, so the words were facing up again. I had originally pictured there being much more excitement sprinkled with some jumping up and down and screaming once I finally typed out the last period, but it was still exciting to know I'd finally accomplished what I set out to do. I wasn't going to let it ruin the thing I spent a year molding into something I could be proud of.

I took one last look over everything and slid my MacBook back into my bag. Finishing my first novel was a cause for celebration. I was going to let myself get one of the more expensive drinks and not feel bad about spending like six dollars on a glorified milkshake.

I grabbed my manuscript and looked up at the line. Maybe I'd wait another few minutes. I glanced back at the glass doors to see if it was still snowing, and caught of glimpse of dark sunglasses, all black clothing, and some brooding, pursed lips. There was only one person that could look that melodramatic on a daily basis. I waved my hand in the air. "Cordelia!"

She lowered her glasses and I thought she was going to turn and walk off in the other direction. She stopped and I saw her shoulders slump down, like she thought she was going to regret deciding to talk to me. She approached me and removed her sunglasses. If anyone was to ever get an award for RBF, it would've been Cordelia.

"Hi, I didn't expect to see you here," I said.

"Well, I was hoping that by coming all the way out here I would be able to avoid seeing anyone I knew. I just wanted a peaceful cup of coffee and to read a good book. Obviously, I was wrong."

"You do realize that I live down the block, right? You were literally on my couch last week."

"I don't know. I thought your entire generation thought they were too cool for chain coffee shops or something."

I set my manuscript back down on the table and put my bag in between my legs. "I think you've been watching too many teen dramas." I studied her face. She didn't look drunk, but something didn't seem right. "How are you doing today?"

"Well, if you must know, I haven't had a drop of alcohol in almost a week, and I've hated every minute of it. So I've been drowning my sorrows in coffee which is actually only making me more fidgety. Oh, and apparently the tumor that's decided to move into my brain is a lot further along than anyone realized, so it's safe to say I'll probably be blind before February. Other than that, I'm great. Thanks for asking."

Suddenly my problems felt so small.

How was I supposed to follow that? I could feel myself looking at her like she was some sort of victim and I didn't know how to stop myself. "So—" I paused. I really had no clue how to steer into a new conversation. "Hung out with Kara lately?"

"This is what we're doing now? Okay. No, I have not 'hung out' with Kara lately. That girl is more annoying than the tumor pushing up against my brain."

"Hey now. That might be going a little too far. She's not that bad."

"Really? The girl who's playing dirty in a competition to see who can get me to sign over movie rights for my book so she can take the editor job isn't that bad?" She peered into my soul. "Yes. I know about that. I'm not stupid, you know."

"How long have you known?"

"Well, it didn't take long for me to figure out something was up when they started sending you two to try and convince me. And I have to say it was really amusing watching you try, but you're both just so bad at it. I talked to Maya and got her to tell me everything."

Her friendship with Maya. I didn't think about that. I didn't think they were really that close.

"Any chance of me convincing you to sign that dotted line? I mean, since you already know everything and all."

Her eyes shifted down toward my manuscript and then back up at me. "Is that the finished piece?"

"Yes."

"Can I read it? And I can hand it back to you with some of my own notes if you want."

I couldn't understand why she was being so nice to me. She had every reason to be angry at the world, and most of the time she was. She had to be playing some sort of game.

"Why?"

"This might be my last chance to critique something before I go completely blind. You can't say no to a dying woman."

"You're really pulling the dying card right now?"

"Why not? I have it so I might as well use it. And you're the only person that knows so you're the only one it'll work on."

I hesitated before sliding it across the table and into her hands. It was much sooner than I had anticipated on sending my baby out into the world like that.

"I'll take good care of it." Cordelia said, no doubt understanding how nervous that whole exchange was making me. "But don't expect me to go soft on you. Just because I know you personally doesn't mean I'm going to sugar coat things for you."

"Of course. I wouldn't expect you to."

She grinned before slipping the stack into her bag to shield it from the snow.

I was beginning to understand why women needed such large purses. It came in handy in case you wanted to guilt someone into giving you the project they spent a year of their life crafting.

She slid her sunglasses back on over her face and stared at me. "Do you really want that position?"

I didn't have an answer, and she knew I didn't. Why was it so difficult for me to figure out what I really wanted? I had a plan, but I couldn't force myself to follow it anymore. It was actually painful to think about it.

Cordelia zipped her coat back up and vanished in between the people running for cover from the blizzard.

chapter **twenty-nine**

The apartment was still disturbingly quiet and empty. Although I could have sworn I heard one of the girls sneak in the night before, shut themselves up in Adrienne's room for a few hours, and then leave again. My money was on it being Zoe catching some shut eye in between shifts at the hospital. I wouldn't want to sleep in one of those on call rooms either.

I've seen *Grey's Anatomy*. I know what goes on in there.

I rolled over on my other side and watched the slow falling through the window. The apocalyptic-like weather had finally gone, but there was still too much snow for me. Living in the city was great, but I wasn't even thinking about all the snow when we decided to move. It made me regret not moving some place warmer, like Florida or Hawaii. Not like those places weren't still an option, though. Everyone was still so angry with me that they probably wouldn't have even noticed or cared if I just fell off the radar.

I pulled myself up just enough to peer over the back of the rolling chair at the clock sitting on my desk. Ten more minutes until I had to get up and start getting ready for work. Twenty if I skipped my shower. Or I could call in. I just wasn't sure if they'd accept *"I don't really feel like adulting today"* as a plausible excuse.

My phone chimed from my bedside table. I craned my neck around, blindly fumbled for it, and tried to read my notifications with the whole one eye closed situation going on.

Three missed calls and a voicemail from Henry and six new texts from Theo.

You on your way?

Dude, where are you? The meeting's about to start.

Seriously, you don't wanna miss this one.

If you get here now, Jonathan might not yell.

Scratch that, the no yelling train has left the station.

Get here now!

"Shit!"

I tore the covers off my body, threw on my glasses, and tailed it to the bathroom after throwing on some presentable-ish clothes I found in my dresser.

No shower for me.

I glanced at myself in the mirror and decided I could fix the train wreck on my head with some water and the hand dryers in the restrooms at work. I snatched my little jar of hair product from the cabinet, threw on my boots, coat, and hat and left a trail of smoke out the door. I raced down the stairs and busted through the front doors of the building.

All I could think about most of the way to work was just how much Jonathan was going to yell at me for being an irresponsible flake. I really should've just called in because I wasn't in any mood to be on the receiving end of a one-sided shouting match.

My phone vibrated against my leg. Part of me was hoping it would be either Adrienne or Zoe wanting to make up so I could have some semblance of how life used to be. The other part just really didn't feel like dealing with any of it. Or maybe it was Theo telling me not to even bother coming in because Jonathan fired me. That would've just been the icing on top of the cake.

Adrienne's name flashed across my screen and I stopped in the middle of the sidewalk.

Someone bumped into me and yelled in my ear as they pushed me aside. "For fuck's sake! Move your ass, dipshit!"

I have a package being delivered today sometime. Just put it in my room and I'll come get it tomorrow.

So, it wasn't a text saying that she wanted to meet up to talk things out so she could come back home, but at least she was talking to me. Progress. And she was still calling it her room, so that was something.

Yeah, no worries. Maybe when you come by we can sit down and talk. I really miss you.
Read 8:33 a.m.

I dashed for the front doors and made a run for it across the lobby to the elevators, nearly knocking over a few people in the process. I crammed myself onto the first elevator that came and tried to calm my breathing as the doors closed. I watched the floor indicator above the door as I made my way up to the office, stopping at nearly every floor before I got there.

There was no sign of Jonathan or Maya waiting for me. I crept across the office and snuck passed Kara, who was hopefully too involved in her work to even notice I just got there. I quietly lowered myself into my seat and logged into my computer.

"Look who finally decided to show up," Kara said.

I peeked over my computer and her eyes were still on her screen. I sunk into my seat and tried to hide behind my monitor.

"You know I can still see you, right? That's not helping literally anything, and you just look stupid right now."

I pulled myself back up and finished logging into everything.

"Noah, where have you been, dude?" Theo asked as he approached my desk.

"Sorry, I was still in bed when you texted me. I didn't even know we had a meeting today. When did that all happen?"

"Everyone should've gotten an email yesterday about it," he said.

I pulled up my email and scrolled through the new messages in my inbox. "I have a hell of a lot of spam messages, but nothing about a meeting."

"Really . . ." Theo trailed off on his sentence and turned his head.

I followed his line of vision to Kara's desk.

"Maya had Kara email everyone in the office yesterday morning about it."

She stopped typing and looked up at us. "What was that?"

"Noah didn't get the email you sent yesterday about the meeting."

"Really? I must have just forgotten to attach you. There's a lot of people in this office. I can't be expected to remember everyone all the time."

"A lot of things seem to be slipping your mind these days," I said.

"I guess I just have a lot on my plate."

Theo couldn't have been buying any of it. Kara had been trying to sabotage me since day one of the competition.

"This is totally all my fault. If Jonathan makes a big deal of it, just send him my way. I'll explain what happened."

"Regardless, Jonathan wants to see you in his office when he gets done with his conference call."

I got up and took a lap around to the other side of my desk. I could feel the frustration boiling up again and I wasn't going to be able to just sit and wait for it to settle this time.

"Kara, can I speak with you in private for a moment?"

"Ooh, I'm like super busy right now. Can this wait until a little later?"

"Uh, actually it can't." I couldn't help but mock her annoyingly bubbly tone. "Can I please see you in the conference room, like now?"

"Oh my, God. Fine. Just give me a second." She finished whatever she was working on and followed me down the hall into the conference room.

I closed the door behind us and leaned against it for a moment. I could feel a knot forming in the pit of my stomach and there was a tingling in my fingertips. I pushed myself away from the door and turned to face Kara.

"What's the issue now?" she asked.

"Seriously? What's the issue?" Breathing was becoming more difficult and the tingling was slowly spreading to my hands and the rest of my arms. "I was able to look passed all the other crap that you pulled. I figured it was all just a little bit of friendly competition, which couldn't really hurt. But this could have cost me my job, Kara! What were you thinking?"

"Oh please. I wasn't gonna let you get fired. Nothing bad was ever going to happen to you."

"That isn't the point! What happened to us? What the hell did I do to you to make you hate me as much as you do?"

She stepped closer and looked me in the eye. "If you have to ask me what you did, then obviously we were never really that good of friends." She pushed passed me and walked out, slamming the door behind her.

My head was reeling, and I grabbed hold of the table for support. My arms were starting to go numb and my heart was pounding wildly against my rib cage.

The last thing I remembered before I woke up in a hospital gown was hoping that Death had finally come to rescue me from my own personal hell on earth. Unfortunately, that was not the case.

I was actually trying to make my brain believe that I was dreaming myself into an episode of *Grey's Anatomy*, which I probably would've believed, given the circumstances, had I not realized how sore the entire right side of my face was.

I pulled the little metal bedside rolling table closer and opened the camera app on my phone. I'd somehow managed to scrape up my face and reopen the gash on my forehead that had just started to disappear.

The door opened and a blonde woman with scrubs and a white coat walked in. The fact that I wasn't dreaming was only solidified by the fact that my doctor wasn't some super hot guy with huge biceps and dimples for days.

"You're awake. I'm Doctor Kaufman, how are you feeling?"

I propped myself up a little more. "What happened? I feel like I had a heart attack or something."

"Your EKG came back normal, so you most definitely did not have a heart attack. By the looks of it, it was a very severe panic attack, which can sometimes feel a lot like a heart attack."

There was a twinge of pain in my head and I rubbed my temple.

"And as for your head, there doesn't appear to be any sign of a concussion or internal damage, but I would like to keep you overnight. Just to be safe."

"How long was I out?"

"Just a few hours."

"A few hours? Oh my, God! My boss is going to murder me." I tried to jump out of bed, but when the room started spinning, I felt like I was going to pass out.

"Whoa, calm down. Everything is fine. It was your boss that found you banged up and wandering around." She looked through the chart in her hands. "A Ms. Maya Reynolds. She wanted me to tell you to take as much time as you needed and that there was no immediate rush to get back to work."

Of course Maya was the one to find me. Why would anything in my life work out the way I wanted it to? No way she would ever consider me for editor now that she'd seen me crumble under pressure firsthand.

"From what we were able to pull together from your medical history, I see that you were diagnosed with Generalized Anxiety Disorder back in 2015. Are you still taking your medication or going to therapy?"

"I stopped both before I moved to the city. I felt like I was learning to handle it on my own, so I didn't really see

249

much of a reason to continue taking it. And who has the time for therapy these days?"

Doctor Kaufman grabbed the little rolling chair and wheeled it to my bedside. She looked me straight in the eye.

Maybe I was in an episode of *Grey's* after all.

"Look, I'm not a native to this city either, so I understand the pressure to want to do everything the New York way and do things on your own. But sometimes we all need to focus on doing what's right for ourselves and our own health, and not worry about what anyone else thinks we should be doing. I'm not telling you that you should go back to medication and therapy, because that's totally up to you. I'm just saying that it's something that should be considered."

"I'll think about it," I finally said.

"Great! Now how about I go find you a more comfortable room for the night?"

While I wasn't too crazy about the thought of staying in the hospital all night and being forced into eating hospital food, it did beat out having to spend yet another night alone in the apartment.

"Sounds good."

She smiled from ear to ear and rolled the chair back to its place under the desk. She pulled open the door and paused. "Looks like you have a visitor."

Maybe it was Death finally sending someone to finish me off.

Adrienne walked through the door.

Nice one, Death.

"How'd you know I was here?"

"Well, I am still your emergency contact . . . so—" She shuffled across the floor and hopped up on the corner of the bed, her feet dangling over the side. She kicked her legs back and forth and stared down at the floor.

I found a piece of string hanging off the blanket they gave me and started playing with it, wrapping it around my finger. Why was it so difficult for me? We'd never had that much of an issue talking through a problem when we had one in the past, so why was I making it so much harder than it needed to be? I just needed rip it off like a Band-Aid.

"I'm so sorry. I shouldn't have said all the things that I did. And I promise I don't think you're using being with your boss as a way to get a raise or something. I was an ass."

"Well, I won't argue with that statement." Adrienne twisted her body around to face me. "I'm the one that should be sorry. I never should have just run out that night. I've been a baby. I should have just been an adult and talked to you about it."

"We both made mistakes. Not just one of us can take the blame for this entire mess."

"Yeah, but most of this is totally on me. I never should have gotten pissy with you for keeping Bennett a secret from me knowing that I'd been keeping Tyler a secret for like seven months."

"Yeah, that was a shitty thing to do. But, regardless, we're adults now and we shouldn't have to tell each other every little detail of our lives. I just care about you, and I don't want you getting hurt. I hate to say it, but one of you is bound to get burned at some point in this situation. It's dangerous."

She turned and started swinging her feet back and forth again. I knew that look anywhere.

"What's wrong? Did something happen?"

"We almost got caught."

"What? When did this happen?"

"The other night. We went out to see a show, and we ran into someone from the school board. We played it off and I don't think they really suspected anything, but it was terrifying, and it got us thinking how stupid we've been to think we could keep it a secret. It's amazing we even made it that far without a close call. So, we got to talking and he decided he's taking another principal position he got offered at a private school."

"Well that's great news. It means you guys don't have to keep sneaking around anymore. You can have a real relationship."

She was still looking down. "Yeah, it's great."

"Okay, why do I seem more excited about this than you do right now?"

She looked up at the ceiling and avoided eye contact. "He wants me to move in with him."

"Oh." I paused. "And is that what you want too?"

"Maybe? I don't know."

I can't say I was exactly thrilled by the possibility of Adrienne moving out. I wanted nothing more than to beg her to stay, but I couldn't hold on forever. We were getting older and she was in love. And I knew that if I asked her not to go, she would eventually resent me. It may not have been any time soon, but it would have happened one day. I needed to make things right.

"Go."

"What?"

"Go. Move in with your man. It was only a matter of time. And I'm sure Zoe will probably be getting back to her life soon. The lease on the apartment is up after this month, so I can find a one bedroom. The apartment is falling apart anyway, and lord knows Derek won't fix anything."

"Are you sure?"

"So sure. I was beginning to think that maybe I'm getting too old to be living with roommates anyway, you know? I need to get out there and spread my wings."

She laughed. "You're so weird."

The door swung open and Zoe rushed in holding a tablet. She closed the door behind her and glared at both of us.

"Howdy," I said.

"What the hell happened? And was I going to get an invitation to this party?" She hopped up on the other side of my bed, which wasn't helping my claustrophobia any.

"It was just a panic attack. I'm fine."

She pointed at the bandages covering parts of my face.

"Okay, well that's just a minor thing. It's not a big deal."

"I'm sorry, sweetie. I would have called you, but I figured you were probably swamped, and I didn't want to disturb you," Adrienne said.

"Is there anything I can get you?" Zoe asked.

"A drink maybe?"

"Ooh, I don't think they have any vodka in the cafeteria."

"Low blow, dude. Some water will be fine."

She jumped up. "Okay, after I finish up my rounds I'll go see if I can get my hands on some ice water for you. I'll be here all night, so just text me if you need anything at all, okay?"

"I will. Thank you for stopping by."

"I should probably head out, too. Tyler's covering for me and I don't know how long he can keep the kids reading Gatsby before there's an attempted coup."

"Love you," Zoe and Adrienne said on their way out the door.

I couldn't tell for sure if everything would go back the way it was before yet, but at least it was all a start in the right direction.

My phone vibrated in my lap and Maya's name popped up.

I wanted to tell you at the meeting, but Cordelia has chosen to sign over the film rights and the holiday party has been moved up to this

Saturday night. The company's next editor will be announced then. Good luck and get better soon.

It was finally over.

chapter **thirty**

"This is it," I whispered to myself as I stood out on the sidewalk staring up.

By the end of the night I would have the answer to what the rest of my career would look like. I would either be picked, which would most likely eventually result in my mind getting overloaded to the point of having another severe panic attack, or I would be overlooked, have to continue working the job I hated for the man I could barely tolerate, and then wind up having a panic attack. Either way I saw another mental breakdown in my future that I may never really recover from.

Maybe I really am just a little too overdramatic sometimes.

I walked through the front doors and headed for the elevators. Kara came into my line of vision and I paused, contemplating whether it would be weird if I waited for another one.

The doors opened and she stepped on. "Are you coming or what?"

Well, at least that debate was settled.

I walked onto the elevator and the doors closed. I took one step closer to the railing and stared straight forward. "Big night, huh?"

"Yup."

"Well, good luck."

"Thanks, but I don't really need any luck," she said with a smile.

I couldn't hold it in any longer, even if I did wind up back in the hospital. "Enough. Why won't you just tell me what your problem is? And don't give me any of that 'you would know if we were ever really friends' crap. I want a real answer right here, right now."

"Oh, so you want to do this now. Fine." She leaned over and pulled the stop button.

When I said I wanted an answer I didn't mean while I was suspended a couple hundred feet in the air by a bunch of cables in a metal box.

"You want to know what my problem is? It's you!"

"Me? What did I ever do to you?"

"Everything was fine when you first got here. I mean, you complained a lot about how much you hate your job. And I mean a lot. But I let it slide. But then you come in here and try to take away the job that you don't even want and that I've been working my ass off to get in the year and a half I've been here. I deserve this win, not you!"

"I didn't know you wanted it that bad."

"And why would you? You were too busy talking about whatever guy you were dating at the time to notice.

Cordelia was right, I did grow up with money, but I don't want to be handed things. I actually really love working for everything I get and knowing that I've earned all of it. After college I basically cut off my entire family and everything I knew. This is all I have and you're just coming in and trying to take it away all because you're too chicken to follow your own dream!"

"Aye, now that's a little far!"

She crossed her arms. "Look, I'm sorry that you were in the hospital and I genuinely hope that you're okay, because that really sucks. And I know you're dealing with a lot of your own stuff right, but I need this way more than you do." She pushed the emergency stop button back in and we started moving again. "This isn't my backup plan like it is for you. This is all I have." The elevator stopped and Kara walked into the party.

I held the door open and looked out at everything. The mingling, the food, the second-rate Christmas tunes. I wasn't ready to face any of it yet. Especially not the deciding vote. I pulled my hand back and let the doors close again. I hit the button for highest floor and rode it all the way up, trying to calm myself down.

When the doors opened again, I headed straight for the staircase that led up to the roof. I could feel the cold air blowing in from underneath the door from the other end of the hallway. The wind hit me in the face at full strength as I forced open the door and stepped out onto the roof.

There was something about the New York skyline at night that helped me regain my cool and clear my head. I stood staring up at the sky, trying to see passed the lights that were drowning out the stars, when I realized I wasn't alone.

"I didn't expect to see you up here," I said.

"Oh hey," Henry said. "I just needed to get out of there for a minute."

"Same." I leaned against the railing next to him and looked out.

"I can go back if you want. I know this is kind of your special place and I don't want to interfere with anything."

"No, you're fine. You can stay. If you want to, I mean."

Would it have been wrong to tell him just how much I really wanted to stay up there with him all night? A friend was totally allowed to say stuff like that to another friend, right? I was so close I was practically inhaling his cologne and it was driving me nuts.

"Tonight's the big night," he said.

"Yeah."

"Are you ready?"

"Honestly, I don't know if I'll ever be ready for any of that down there." I ran my fingers through a small pile of snow on the ledge.

"Why didn't you call me?" Henry asked.

"Huh?"

"When you were in the hospital. Why didn't you tell me you were there?

"It wasn't really a big deal."

"It would have been nice to know that my b—my friend—was lying in a hospital bed. Instead I had to hear it through the grapevine the next day when you didn't show up for work two days in a row."

He had no idea how much I enjoyed him almost using the b word. It gave me some hope, even if it was just false hope.

"It was nothing. It was just a panic attack, and I didn't want to worry you over nothing. Honestly it's a little embarrassing."

Henry turned his head and studied the right half of my face, which was now bruised up, and my forehead had a butterfly closure strip. "Really? That's nothing?"

"It looks much worse than it is. You should have seen me like two days ago. It was just one big bruise and my face was so swollen I could barely open my eye. Believe me when I say that *this* is nothing."

We gazed out at the city together in silence for a few minutes. A drunk band of college-aged kids fumbled down the streets. Their laughs were barely audible above the noise of the city, but hearing what I did was enough to remind me of when that was me and all my friends from school. Back when I didn't have to worry whether or not I would be scheduling meetings for Jonathan for the rest of my professional life.

Henry took a deep breath. "I guess after tonight it's all over. Life can finally go back to normal."

"I don't even know what normal is anymore." I pulled up my collar and shoved my hands inside my pockets. "Do you think I should take it?"

"What do you mean?"

"If it's me, do you think I should accept the job?"

Henry pressed his back up against the railing. "I don't think I'm exactly the right person to be giving you advice on that."

"But if you had to give me an answer? This is all in the event that I am the one to be picked."

"Well, if I really have to answer this for you, I'd say you should just do whatever it is your gut is telling you to do."

"You know, you're really no help."

"I'm just saying that you need to do whatever you feel is right for you and stop worrying so much about whatever everyone else thinks you should do."

Why had my life suddenly become an episode of *Full House*?

"That's the same advice Doctor Kaufman gave me."

Henry looked at me funny. "Who?"

"Never mind." I shivered and started to pull Henry in closer for extra warmth before I remembered the whole "friends" conversation. "We should probably get back down there. It's getting pretty cold up here."

"And I'm sure Maya's looking for you."

"Hmm—don't remind me."

By the time we got back downstairs to the party, majority of the food was gone and there weren't any good songs left to play. Given there were even any good songs to begin with.

We took off our coats and hung them up on the little coat rack they put up for the night.

"Nice sweater," I said, staring at what looked like an image of Rudolph that Christmas had thrown up all over. "I must have missed the ugly Christmas sweater memo."

"Just trying to be festive."

"Right."

We wove in and out of people, most of which I had never seen before, looking for Maya. When we finally did find her, she was surrounded by Jonathan, Theo, Kara, Cordelia, and some random middle-aged dude in a hot shot suit.

"Noah, I'm so glad you could make it!" Maya said. She winced at the sight of the bruises on my face. "How are you feeling?"

"A lot better today thankfully."

"I'm glad to hear that. Noah, I would like you to meet Drew Conrad, the production president at Fox Studios. He's here for the holidays so I figured I'd invite him to come and enjoy the party."

"It's nice to meet you, Mr. Conrad."

He shook my hand firmly. "Please, call me Drew. Noah, was it?"

"Yes."

"It's nice to meet you, Noah."

I shifted my body in Cordelia's direction. "I didn't expect to see you here tonight."

"Well, I did have a lot to do with the main event tonight, so why wouldn't I?"

Maya cupped her hands. "Speaking of which, I think it's time now that everyone's here." She set her cup down on the closest desk and straightened out the wrinkles in her dress before heading up to the front of the office so everyone could see her. "Excuse me, can I have everyone's attention please?" She turned off the music.

I was getting physically sick and I could feel my heart rate speeding up. She hadn't even announced it yet and I felt like I was on the verge of another panic attack.

"I hope everyone is having a good time. There is still some food in the back I see, so feel free to dig in and finish it off. Take some home, I don't care. I just don't want it here when we come back Monday morning. The night is still young, so I promise I will let everyone get back to their fun, but first I have an announcement I'd like to make."

The tightness in my chest was returning and I could feel myself struggling to breath. Without thinking, I latched onto Henry's arm and my face went hot. I couldn't see it, but I was sure it was a visible shade of red. I let go and glued my hand to my side.

His hand brushed up against my sweaty palm, and the next thing I knew, our fingers were intertwined. It wasn't enough to completely cure my anxiety, but it helped calm me down and cut the chances of another panic attack in half.

"As you all know, we recently had two spots for editor come open, and our lovely Theo here graciously stepped in to fill one of those rolls, but that still left one spot open. Over the past few weeks, two of our top assistants, Kara Lynch and Noah Carlisle, have been competing for the spot, and while they both bring their own strengths to the table and are equally deserving of this role, we can only choose one."

I squeezed his hand even tighter, sure I would wind up cutting off his circulation if Maya didn't hurry up with the announcement. He just stood there and let me do it. I glanced at Kara, who was clutching onto Theo for dear life.

"So, without further ado, please join me in welcoming the newest addition to the editorial staff at Hale Publishing, Noah Carlisle."

It took me a minute to pull myself back to reality and realize that Maya called my name.

I did it. I mean, I actually did it.

Everyone was still clapping for me when I realized Maya had been motioning for me to join her. I didn't even know if I'd be able to get the words out.

The adrenaline was still pumping through my body when I let go of my hold on Henry's hand. "Wow, thank you so much for this opportunity. This is—just—" I caught a glimpse of Kara's face. She was totally crushed, and all of it was my fault. Everything she said to me in the elevator was flashing through my memory. And then I remembered everything that Henry and Cordelia said to me about doing what was right for me. For the first time, I understood what they meant. "This is such an honor. And you have no idea how much I appreciate getting this opportunity but—no."

There was an audible gasp, and several looks of confusion amongst the masses. Kara included.

"Excuse me?" Maya said.

I searched through the crowd and set my gaze on Cordelia. She seemed extremely satisfied with my abrupt no.

"I can't take this job."

"Uh, everyone please return to your regularly scheduled evening." Maya switched the music back on. "Noah, can I please speak with you in my office?"

I felt like I was being called into the principal's office when she used that tone.

Maya led me into her office and closed the door behind me. She approached me and folded her arms. It was her oddly intimidating power move. That and the glare that could likely get information out of a terrorist if she was put in the situation.

"What was that?"

"I'm sorry. I'm just not the right person for this job."

"What do you mean? I wouldn't have given it to you if you weren't."

"No, I'm really not."

She walked around to the other side of her desk and sank into her chair. "If this has anything to do with the hospitalization, I completely understand, and I meant it when I told you that I won't hold that against you."

"I know you did. And thank you for that. It's nice to see the company taking mental health seriously."

"You're one of the best workers this company has ever seen, Noah. I see great things happening for you here."

I took the seat opposite her. "And I really do appreciate everything that you've done for me, but I can't take this position."

Maya leaned forward over her desk. "And you do understand that if you pass this up, I can't guarantee that another spot will open up any time soon. It could be another year. Maybe more."

"Yes, I understand. But I think it's time for me to go home."

"That sounds like a plan. Go home, relax, and then come back on Monday refreshed and ready to work."

"Actually, I mean all the way home. Back to Illinois."

"I can't let you do that, Noah. I will deny it if anyone asks, but we need you here. You're an asset to this company."

I traced my fingers along the edge of the desk. "It took recent events to help me realize this isn't what I want. It never really was. I think it's time that I stepped aside and let someone who really wants this job have it."

Maya took a deep breath and leaned back in her chair. She looked me in the eye. "Here's what I'm gonna do. I'm going to give you some time off, and I want you to go home for a while. Spend time with your family, relax, and just get your head back on straight. I expect to see you back here in the new year refreshed and ready to start your new job as editor. Consider it an early Christmas present."

Later that night, I packed a bag and was ready to hit the road to the airport. I threw my duffel bag over my shoulder and wheeled my case out into the kitchen.

I opened my text thread with Brooke.

Are you sure you want to do this?

Yes, I replied.

Okay. I sent the money to your Venmo. The flight should be leaving at around 10:15, so don't miss it. I'll be there to pick you up. You know Mom isn't gonna be too thrilled about all of this, Brooke texted.

Well then Mom's just gonna have to get over it. I'm leaving for the airport soon. I'll see you when I get there.

Okay. Have a safe flight. I love you.

Love you too.

I looked around the apartment one last time and couldn't believe that chapter of my life was coming to an end. The thought of leaving everything behind that I'd built was a difficult one to process, but I knew my time was up and I needed to leave while my life was still being held together by tiny threads.

I looked down at my phone again and did the only thing I had left to do. I scrolled through my messages and pulled up the group chat between Zoe, Adrienne, and I to write the first message in quite a while.

I've been doing a lot of thinking, and I think it's time for me to go home. My time is up and there's nothing left me for here. Please don't be upset. This is something I need to do for myself. Adrienne, I can only imagine how small Tyler's place is with him being a bachelor, so the apartment is all yours. Move in, start a family, and be happy. I really do wish both of you the very best that life and this city has to offer. I love you both.

I switched my phone off and shoved it back into my pocket before I left for the airport.

chapter **thirty-one**

I'd been back home for a week and I still found it strange to be waking up in my old high school bedroom again.

It was especially difficult to get used to having a twin-size bed again, which I managed to almost fall out of nearly every night, as well as waking up to a huge poster for the final *Deathly Hallows* film staring me in the face. All of it reminded me how far I'd come since high school. I still really enjoyed things like *Harry Potter* and playing The Sims for hours on end, but I was so far from the person I was back then, and I was so grateful for that.

I threw my covers off and leapt out of bed. I slipped into a pair of sweatpants and my slippers and ran downstairs, following the scent of freshly cooked bacon.

My mom was flipping a pancake over the stove. "Good morning."

"That smells so good."

One of the things that I missed most about being home was Mom's cooking. Sure, I knew how to cook a decent meal, but half the time I was so busy in the city that I barely had time to grab a bottle of water for breakfast. It was nice to actually have a home cooked meal for a change.

Brooke popped up from behind me holding a small box wrapped in ribbon. "Well good morning, Sleeping Beauty. I've been here for an hour waiting for you to get up." She shoved the box into my chest. "Merry Christmas."

"Okay . . . ow."

"Oh, don't be a baby."

Mom led us to the table where she already had plates of eggs, sausage, bacon, and biscuits set out. I could feel my mouth already starting to water in anticipation. She set down the pancakes and I started piling food onto my plate.

"Open it," Brooke said.

"It's so pretty though. I don't want to mess it up."

"Oh my, God. Just do it or I'll do it for you."

I carefully untied the ribbon and removed the lid from the box. "Oh. A tie. You shouldn't have."

"Okay, captain sarcasm. It was originally meant for your first day on the job as editor, but I guess now it can function as a job search tie."

"Sounds great." I set the box down and took a bite of my chocolate chip pancakes.

"You are going to get a job soon, right?"

"I guess."

"And you're really not planning on going back?"

"I don't see it happening any time soon. So, for the time being, that's gonna be a no."

"Brooke, just lay off your brother, okay? It's Christmas."

We ate in silence for a few minutes. All I could hear were the sounds of forks scraping against plates and excessive amounts of chewing.

"So, you're not going back and you're not looking for a job? What exactly do you plan to do then?"

"Brooke, I said drop it."

"No. I've sat here and watched him mope around for over a week. I know you hit a rough patch, and I feel for you, but you can't sit around here feeling sorry for yourself anymore. You need to get off your ass and get back out there. I hoped you would get out there and do something with your life and not be trapped here like every other sad sap."

Mom gave her the dirtiest look.

"No offense, Mom. But you have to admit you wanted him to get out of here too."

I wanted to see myself get out of Illinois too. It was the state where next to nothing happened unless you were actively going to Chicago all the time to look for a life. I had no interest in that. And as much as I missed New York and the excitement of it all, I wasn't sure if I actually fit in there anymore.

There was a knock at the front door.

"Are either of you expecting anyone?" Mom asked.

"Nope."

"And no one from here knows that I'm back as far as I know," I said.

Mom sat up and headed to answer the door.

I shoveled another mouthful of pancake into my mouth and took a sip of my milk while avoiding Brooke's death glares. She could have competed with Cordelia in the scary looks department.

"Have you at least been writing at all since you've been home?"

"No, but I did finish my manuscript a couple weeks before I left."

"That's awesome! What are you gonna do with it?"

"Actually, I gave it to someone for them to read. They never got back with me, so I can really only assume it was terrible."

I didn't expect anything else. Cordelia had her own issues to worry about. I was likely at the very bottom of her list of important things to do, especially if my book sucked.

Mom wandered back into the kitchen and placed her hands on the back of her chair. "It's for you, Noah."

I tried peeking around the corner to get a view of the door. "Who is it?"

"Just go."

I wiped a little bit of chocolate from my pancake off my face with a napkin and stood up. I rounded the corner and walked down the hall toward the living room. I stopped in the doorway when I saw the familiar head of blonde hair standing in my family's living room looking at all our photos.

"Zo, you're here."

"We've all been trying to get ahold of you for days," she said. Her back was still turned.

"I've had my phone off since I left. I just haven't really felt like being yelled at for leaving." I leaned up against the arm of the couch. "Not that I'm not happy to see you, but what are you doing here?"

Zoe continued walking around, looking at old family photographs. "It's funny. I rehearsed what I was going to say the entire plane ride and then the entire car ride. And now that I'm here, I'm totally blanking."

I slid off the arm and settled into one of the cushions. "You don't have to rehearse anything. It's just me."

She stopped walking and finally turned to face me, though she seemed to be avoiding any real eye contact at all costs. She examined the marks on my face. "Your face is looking a lot better. Although the one on your forehead worries me a little bit. Have you been putting any antibiotic ointment on it?"

I grabbed her hand and pulled it away from my face. "Zoe, what is it? I know you didn't come all this way just to look at my face."

I finally caught her gaze and she sat down.

"I'm sorry. I'm sorry for all of it. The drinking and just not being a very good friend."

"Hey, that's in the past now. It's fine, we don't have to talk about that anymore."

"But I need to. I haven't been totally honest with you about what happened between me and Jordan and why we ended things. I've been going to therapy for the last few weeks, and I think I'm finally ready to talk about what happened."

"I swear, if he hurt you, I'll—"

"No, he didn't hurt me, but thank you." She paused and I could already see her eyes getting glossier. "I was pregnant. I was gonna be a mom."

I just sat there looking at her. I didn't know what to say or how to react.

"I didn't want to get my hopes up, let alone tell anybody. I had a doctor tell me once that my chances of even conceiving weren't great. So, I figured I'd wait just a little while before I said anything. Regardless, he started getting super excited and started picking out baby clothes and he convinced me to pick out names and stuff. Eventually I got really into it too and, of course, I got my hopes up."

The tears started streaming down her face and I grabbed her hand.

"One night I was working one of my longer shifts and I got this really bad pain in my stomach. It felt like someone was just squeezing as hard as they could. Finally it got so bad that I had to go get it checked out and—and I—" She collapsed into my arms and struggled to catch a breath. "It hurts so bad, Noah."

"I'm so sorry. If I'd known—"

The truth is I didn't really know what I would have done had I known about it. I wasn't prepared for something like that. I couldn't imagine how difficult it must have been for her to go through that.

"I just couldn't deal with the pain anymore and I wanted something else to think about. Literally anything else. I didn't think that a couple of drinks here and there would hurt anything. Eventually a couple led to drinking every night. I wouldn't even let him touch me. He left, and it's all my fault."

I pulled her in tighter. "None of that is your fault, Zo."

She pulled herself out of my grasp and wiped her face dry with the sleeve of her sweater. "Yes, it is. I pushed him away. This is all on me and no one else."

"No, he made his choice to leave. That had nothing to do with you and you can't blame yourself for any of it. This stuff happens, and it takes a while to get through it. If he doesn't get that, then forget him. I'm here for you for anything you need. And so is Adrienne."

She laughed again and did another lap around the living room. "Adrienne's been so busy the last week moving into Tyler's that she's barely had time to talk after I told her all of this."

"So, she didn't take the apartment then? More room for you when you get back, I guess. Although it's kind of a piece of shit place, so I'd move if I were you."

Zoe stopped and leaned over the back of the couch. "Actually, I'm not going back."

"Come again?"

"I quit my job and I'm moving back in with my parents for a while."

"Why aren't you going back?"

"Let's be real, Noah. New York is beautiful, but it's so not the place for me. I don't belong there like you do. You can take the girl out of the country, but you can't take the country out of the girl."

"Of course you belong there."

"I knew I didn't belong there the moment I stepped off the plane, dude. I just went there because you guys were going, and I thought I'd be able to find something new. All I found was the fact that I don't fit in. I never have and I never will." She nuzzled her head onto my shoulder. "You could always take the apartment for yourself, you know."

"Me? No way."

"Oh, come on. Now you're just being stupid. You know you don't belong in a small town like this. I've never seen you more alive than you are when you're there. That's your city. You *are* New York, Noah. And you're kidding yourself if you think you don't belong."

I stood and examined the old pictures sitting on top of the electric fireplace. All of them were taken back when I was in high school, back before my dad decided to tear our family apart. To anyone else, they were photos of the All-American family with a mother, a father, a son, and a daughter.

When I looked at them, I remembered how trapped I felt. I loved my family, but I hated the shell of a person the small town community forced me to become. Once I got to New York, I felt a sense of freedom I'd never experienced before. I was free to become anything I wanted to be, and the sky was the limit. Maybe it really was time for me to stop being such a baby.

"But what about you? I don't want to leave you here all alone," I said.

"You've had your alone time. So now I think it's time for mine. I promise you I'll be fine."

A car horn went off outside and the neighbor's dog went berserk.

"And that would be my dad. He's not really into the whole patience thing sometimes."

"Thank you."

She pulled me in for one last hug. "Any time." She smiled and walked to the door. "Oh, by the way, you might want to turn your phone back on. You'll thank yourself later."

I charged up the living room stairs and into my room. I snatched my phone off the bedside table and powered it on. Almost a hundred text messages, thirty-seven missed calls, and a dozen voicemails. I went through all of them, but the one that caught my attention was the final voicemail from Maya at 7pm the previous night.

"Hi, Noah. I don't know if you've been getting any of these messages, but we really hope you're doing alright, and we miss you. Please call me as soon as you get this.

Cordelia slipped me a copy of your manuscript, and I would like to speak with you."

Did that really just happen?

I flicked my head around to my laptop sitting on top of the desk. I picked it up and carried it to my bed. Opening it, I started searching for anything I could find on Cordelia and her mysterious past. Old interviews, articles, anything really. I figured I had a one in a million shot of finding what I was looking for, but I had to give it a chance.

After what felt like forever, I found an old, archived article about her first divorce from a man named Dean Thompson, a literary agent. I scrolled down and eventually found a mention of a son named Neil.

Luckily for me, most agents had some sort of online presence, so I took the name Dean Thompson to Instagram and voila, he was one of the first few accounts. Most of his posts were all about his clients and book releases and stuff, but after swiping through for a few moments, I found a picture that looked a little too out of place. I tapped on it and hoped I was getting closer. I clicked on the tagged people, and there he was. Neil Thompson, a licensed clinical psychologist residing in Westchester county.

I inhaled deeply before hitting send message.

chapter **thirty-two**

I never thought I'd be back.

I mean, I knew I'd wind up back in New York to visit someday. I fell in love with it the moment I stepped foot on the ground and saw how much life the city had (although I could've done without the smells and trash everywhere). I just never thought I'd be standing outside Hale Publishing again, or any other publishing house for that matter.

As I looked up at the building for the thousandth time, it felt like my first day on the job all over again when I was still seeing everything through rose colored glasses. I took a deep breath and pushed through the doors into the main lobby. I'd taken the trip from the front doors to the elevators more times than I could count, but this time it all felt different. It was nerve-racking and exciting at the same time. I finally understood how our prospective authors felt walking into their first meeting with the company.

I squeezed onto the elevator and waited for the doors to close. My heart was pumping, and I took in a few deep, calming breaths in the attempt to avoid having an anxiety attack. Not even being back on my medication was enough to help me process everything like a normally functioning human being.

When I reached the seventh floor, it was only me and some older guy left on the elevator. I paused for a moment and put my hand over the door to keep it from closing on me. This was actually happening. It all still felt like some sort of weird dream and I was sure I'd wake up soon still in my twin bed back home.

"You going or staying, kid? I've got places to be."

"Sorry." I moved my hand and stepped out.

I realized just how much I really missed the hustle and bustle of the city the closer I got to the center of it all. Everything back home ran way too slow for my taste. The only thing I didn't miss was the traffic and it taking twenty minutes just to go two miles away.

My old desk was still exactly the way I left it. Name plate and all.

Kara was leaning up against her desk, her arms folded tightly against her chest. No doubt something that she picked up from working with Maya for so long. "Maya wanted to leave everything the way it was. Just in case you did come back."

"I take it that since your stuff is still out here, you didn't take the job."

"Oh, no I took it. I earned that shit. My new office didn't get repainted this weekend like it was supposed to, so I'm still out here until Monday. I guess I don't really mind, though. This bad boy got me through a lot this last year and a half. It's gonna be weird not being out here anymore."

"Tell me about it."

Kara pushed herself forward. "Noah, I need to apologize."

"I should be the one apologizing."

"Your words, not mine." She laughed. "But really. I'm sorry for the way I acted. I got a little carried away with the competition, and I'm not proud of some the things I did and said."

"It's okay. I get it. I should have paid more attention to how hard you were working for the job. I'm sorry."

"Well thank you. I appreciate that. I'm just happy it's all over with and everything can finally just go back to normal," Kara said.

"Well, as normal as things can be around here. Just do me a favor and promise you won't let the power of being editor go to your head."

Kara wrapped her arm around my shoulders and walked me down the hall. "Oh, Noah. You know me so much better than that. I can't promise anything."

When Maya told me that she wanted me to talk, I figured she meant just her and I in her office. I wasn't expecting half the staff. Kara opened the door and motioned me inside. Maya, Jonathan, Theo, Henry, and Cordelia were all sitting around the table.

"Noah, I'm glad you could join us. Please take a seat."

I made my way to the other end of the table and wedged into the open seat between Kara and Henry.

Maya reached into her bag and pulled out a binder. She opened it and slipped out a large stack of papers and my manuscript. "You've sat in on dozens of these meetings, so we'll just cut straight to the point. Cordelia was kind enough to let me—or rather all of us—read your manuscript." She laid her hand down on top of it. "I want to publish this story. Everyone in this room thinks it's amazing."

Jonathan just had to chime in. "It was okay. There were some issues that need to be fixed, but definitely not the worst thing I've read."

"What Jonathan is trying to say is that this story has a lot of potential to be something great. And, if you'll let me, I would really love to take a chance on this book."

I was too lost for words. If this was some sort of joke they were playing on me to get me to come back to the office, I wasn't laughing. "I—I don't—" I started fidgeting in my seat and wiped my palms dry on my pants.

Kara latched onto my hand.

"If you choose to sign, because ultimately it is your choice, you will have total creative freedom." Maya sent the stack of papers down the line until they reached me. "You will see in the contract that Jonathan and I worked together to create that this is an offer you won't get anywhere else. You will have final say in whether or not something gets added or removed, what the cover looks like, font, size, all of it. I want you to feel comfortable during the entire process."

I'd helped out with enough proposals and seen enough contracts in my time as Jonathan's assistant to know that the one they were offering me was a good one. I still couldn't help but feel like I was going to crack at any second.

"This is everything you've been waiting for," Kara whispered to me.

"There is one other thing to discuss," Maya said. "But I think I'll let Cordelia take the reins on this one."

That was new. I'd never seen an author get involved in another writer's contract signing before.

"When you gave me your manuscript, I was blown away. And I knew you'd need a push in the right direction. So, I made two copies; I kept the original for myself and I gave one of the copies to Maya. If you'll look in that stack in front of you, you will find a second contract. I handed the third copy to my new connections over at Fox Studios. Once I threatened to pull my support of the film adaption for *The Getaway*, they wasted no time in reading it. And as I suspected they would, they fell in love with it."

I thumbed through the stack, and she was right. I was going to be sick. It was all so much so fast.

"They were very adamant about working with you, Noah," Cordelia said. "But there is a catch to it."

I knew there had to be one somewhere. There was always a catch.

"They want you there in Los Angeles for pre-production every step of the way. Script writing, casting, scouting for locations, all of it. And they want you there as soon as possible."

"But it hasn't even been published," I finally managed to say.

"It's actually not uncommon for film studios to show interest in adapting a manuscript for the screen before it even reaches publication," Maya said.

I kept thumbing through the contracts. "How long does pre-production last?"

"I'd say typically eight or nine months maybe? Could be more though, it just depends. It would be long enough for the book to go through edits and be pushed to publication before they even start filming. Should you choose to sign on with us and be our newest author, you will be working with Kara. Seems only fitting that the two of you should do your first book together. You can work mostly through Skype or email. In person when we can get her there or get you back here."

Again, if it was some sort of practical joke, it wasn't funny at all. It was a lot for one person to take in all at once. I felt Henry's fingers weave into mine.

"What do I do?" I whispered.

"This is everything you've been working for. And you can't let anything stop you from reaching your full potential. Not me. Not anyone. This is your time."

Kara and Henry had a point. This was something that I needed to finally do for myself. I couldn't just keep sitting around back home feeling sorry for myself all the time. I was meant for something so much more than working a shift at McDonald's or the local ma and pa grocery store down the road, just to come home to the silence at the end of it all wishing I could escape from the prison I built myself.

But, jumping into a situation like that when I didn't know if I'd wind up falling on my face while everything burned around me was terrifying. I hadn't planned for any of it. It physically made me sick, but if I did fall, at least I would know I actually tried for once in my life.

I let go of Henry and Kara's hands, picked up the pen beside the stack of contracts, and signed on the dotted lines. The first step toward my new reality. After I finished signing, I looked up to see a smile on Maya's face. If my eyes weren't playing tricks on me, I thought I saw Jonathan smiling too.

"I think this is cause for celebration. Dinner on me tonight," Maya said. She grabbed me by the hand. "I'd stay and talk, but Jonathan and I have some work to do."

"I understand."

"Congratulations. I'm so proud of you."

Jonathan held out a hand for me. "Good work, Carlisle."

I shook it in disbelief. "Thank you, sir."

Maya and Jonathan gathered up their things and left the room.

"We're all gonna go grab some coffee. You want to come?" Theo asked.

"Sure. Just give me a minute."

"No problem. We'll meet you out there." Theo gave me a high five on his way out with Henry and Kara.

I closed the door behind them and faced Cordelia.

"Congrats. This is a big step."

"You really pulled a fast one on me giving that to Maya."

"Well, I just thought I might as well do something decent. Rack up some good karma before I kick the bucket and all."

I ambushed her with a hug, despite her initial fight against it. "Thank you."

"It was nothing. Just thought I'd try to help out." She quit struggling and started patting my back. She didn't seem all that used to affection of any kind, which I was determined to change.

"Are you kidding? It was everything." I pulled away and dug a folded picture out of my pocket. "I didn't know how to thank you, so I started doing some research after I got the voicemails from Maya. I know you're probably gonna be mad, but I did some digging and . . . I found your son." I handed her the photo. "He wants to see you. His number is on the back."

She took it from my hand and tears started streaming down her face when she opened it up. "Is this—"

"Your granddaughter."

"She's so beautiful." She broke down crying and pulled me in for a hug this time. "Thank you so much."

epilogue

It had been just over a year since my last visit, but it was nice being back in New York. Weird for sure, but still nice.

Don't get me wrong, Los Angeles was awesome with all the sunshine and being able to go to the beach at almost any time of the day (given I wasn't too busy trying to make sure the producers and writers didn't completely ruin my vision). I'd also never been more stress free despite the fact that I really wanted to rip out my hair several times a day, but there was nothing like New York in September.

It felt more like home than L.A. or Illinois ever did.

It was 9:30am when the car Maya arranged to have pick me up from my hotel pulled up outside the Fifth Avenue Barnes and Noble. I took a couple deep breaths and gazed out my window.

"We're here, Mr. Carlisle," the driver said as we slowed to a stop.

"Thank you, Marvin. And please call me Noah." I opened the door and prepared myself for the rest of my day.

"Good luck, Noah."

"Thank you. I'm gonna need it." I closed the back door and watched as he drove away.

I couldn't even believe what I was seeing. I pictured it to be a large location, but I never thought it would be that big. Downtown L.A. had nothing on New York, that was for sure. I was just surprised that in my almost full year in the city, I'd never gotten around to making it to a Barnes and Noble. It was probably for the best though. I'd have gone bankrupt a week in.

"Well, don't we look fancy."

"Adrienne! You made it!" I grabbed her by the arms and wrapped her up tight. "I missed you so much, you have no idea."

"I think I have a pretty good idea. You're cutting off my air supply right now, so if you could just—like—oh—"

"Sorry." I loosened my grip, taking a step back to get a good look at her in her little yellow sun dress. Her skin was at least two shades darker. "You look so great. I'd say someone enjoyed her summer off."

"You have no idea. It was nice having someone spoiling me for once."

I smiled, glancing over the top of her head at the line leading to the front doors of the building. It wasn't until that moment that I'd noticed it was wrapped around the block. "Damn. Is there another event going on here during my signing? That's a shit ton of people."

She peeked over her shoulder. "Uh, sorry to burst your bubble, but I think all those people are here for you."

"No way."

"Yes way."

I surveyed the crowd again, this time making eye contact with several people in the process, some of which were beginning to point in my direction. "What is even happening right now?"

"I think you're kind of famous now," she said, grinning up at me. "We should probably get inside. I think some of these people are starting to recognize your face and I don't feel like being trampled right now."

"Okay, I wouldn't go that far," I replied. "I'm not Taylor Swift."

"You're right. You could never be that cool."

I let out a laugh. "Oh shutup." I wrapped my arm around Adrienne's and we snaked our way through the crowd into the building. The first thing I saw was a huge poster of my head and the book's cover. "That's a little creepy."

"It looks like they finally got the size of your head accurate though."

"Oh my gosh. You're so funny. You should really think about going into comedy." We walked around the store, ogling the book displays, finally stopping at the table they had set up for me at the center of the room. "Oh look, another billboard of my face. Right next to where I'll be sitting. With my actual face."

"Is it just me, or do the eyes follow you?"

"It is most definitely not just you. Think they'll notice if I move it a little?"

"I mean, it's your book signing, so I'd say you should be able to do anything you want with it."

I tiptoed passed a couple of workers putting on some finishing touches and nudged my giant head display a few inches out of my view. "That's a little better. If anyone says a word about that, I'm blaming you."

"You're so annoying." Adrienne sunk down into my chair and propped her feet up on the table.

Some kid in a suit who looked about seventeen years old tapped me on the shoulder from behind. "Mr. Carlisle, I was just coming to see if there was anything I could get you. A water, or maybe some Starbucks?"

I looked him up and down. "I'm gonna take a guess here that you're Maya's new assistant. Kyle, right?"

"Kyler, actually. But the name thing happens all the time."

"Is Maya here yet?"

"Yes, she's in the back talking with the manager about last minute details. So, is that a no on the Starbucks?"

"I'm all good here. Thank you for the offer though."

"Actually," Adrienne chimed in, "if it isn't too much trouble, I'll take a venti pink drink."

"Coming right up." Kyler forced out a *"I really hate my job would someone please kill me"* smile and walked back outside.

"Really?"

"What? Someone better take advantage of your new assistant, who by the way looks like he should be in one of my freshman classes instead of being here."

"He isn't my assistant. Maya gave him to me for the day. I told her I didn't want any of this special treatment. The personal driver, the suite at the hotel, the personal assistant. It's all way too much."

She took her feet off the table and sat up straight. "Well, I think you deserve it. It's your first book, so have fun with it. You made this day happen, so enjoy it and stop whining about all the free shit. If you don't want it, I'll take it."

I didn't think it was possible, but being in L.A. actually made me more resistant to letting other people do things for me. Over there, people actually gave things away if they thought you were someone important, which really weirded me out and made me kind of uncomfortable.

Adrienne took out her phone and started scrolling. "Hey, have you heard from Zoe yet? Her plane was supposed to land like an hour ago and I'm getting a little worried that I haven't heard anything yet."

"I take it she never talked to you. She's not coming today."

"What? Why?"

"I had a layover in Chicago yesterday on my way back, so I thought it would be nice to have some lunch together. She has so much going on right now with work and everything, so I just told her not to worry about it. I have a book signing coming up there soon anyway, so she can just go to that one."

"Well, I was hoping we could all get together tomorrow night and hang out like old times, but I guess that's fine." She set her phone down on the table. "How was she when you saw her?"

"She seemed really good. I've never seen her that full of life. She's close enough to the city that she can ride in on the train for work every day, but also far enough away that she still has plenty of open space around home, so she doesn't feel so trapped. I think she's in a good headspace right now."

"Good. Did she mention any guys or anything?"

"No, I think she's just enjoying the freedom right now." I leaned against the edge of the table. "Speaking of guys, how are things with Tyler?"

She stood and wandered around, stopping to pick up a copy of my book to thumb through it. "Things are pretty good. By the way, do you have any plans for April 24th already?"

"That's kind of an oddly specific question. Why do you ask?"

Adrienne reached into her shoulder bag and pulled something out of the front pocket. She slid it onto her finger and held her hand up to my face.

"Oh my—how—what—when did—it's huge!"

"Apparently it belonged to his grandmother, and she had really expensive taste."

"I'll say!" I couldn't even blink. My eyes were getting so dry I thought they were going to fall out of my head. "Is he like secretly some prince or something and you're just not telling me?"

"I wish. Apparently his family's really well off though."

"When did this happen?"

"A few days ago. I thought about FaceTiming you as soon as it happened, but I really wanted to tell you in person."

I pulled her in, squeezing her tight. "I'm so happy for you. That entire weekend I'm yours for whatever you need."

"Good. I have a feeling I'm gonna be a bridezilla. I'm already getting a little grouchy from planning, and I've barely even started."

"Whatever you need, I've got your back. But the second you start throwing things, I'm out."

"Fair enough."

The sound of heels clacking against the linoleum floor echoed from behind me.

"Okay, people. Only ten minutes until showtime. Let's look alive."

That definitely wasn't Maya's voice. I turned and saw Kara standing in front of me wearing a little black dress, fresh golden locks, and a newfound confidence. "Kara— you're blonde. Did you have that during our skype session two days ago, or am I just going crazy?"

"I did not. This whole look happened yesterday."

"Well, it looks really good on you," I replied.

"Thank you. That crowd out there is nuts."

"I know! I wasn't expecting any of it. I know that Cordelia did a lot of tweeting about the book before—"

I'd been so busy the last couple of months I'd almost forgotten. We hadn't all been together much since the funeral. It was still weird to imagine a world where she wasn't around all the time bossing everyone around.

"She'd be proud of how far you've come, Noah."

"I just wish she were here to see all of it."

"I know she's drinking a martini and watching everything you're doing," Kara said, laughing. "Have you seen Maya?"

"No, but she's still in the back going over last-minute details, I think. Also, I have the first few chapters of the next book finally if you wanted to stop by the hotel later and grab them."

"I've actually been meaning to talk to you about that." She ran a hand through her hair. "From here on out any chapters you have will be directed to Theo once he gets back from his time off."

"Don't tell me you're already getting tired of working with me."

"Of course not. I love working with you on your stuff, you know that. Recently the editor-in-chief at our London office just up and quit, so they need someone to help them get things running again. And Maya referred me for the job."

I felt really bad for thinking it, but I was sure Maya just threw Kara under the bus. She hadn't even been an editor for very long, and she was already up for editor-in-chief at the European location? I couldn't have been the only one thinking how disastrous all of that could become in a very short amount of time.

Regardless, after everything that happened between us and the amount of time it took to get our relationship back, I needed to be supportive.

"Wow," I finally said.

"I know, I was shocked too. But Jonathan's been teaching me the ropes, and I think I'm getting the hang of it. I leave for London in three weeks."

"How are you and Theo gonna make this distance thing work?"

"It'll be rough, but we'll get through it."

"Well I'm happy for you. Congratulations."

"Thank you so much."

I turned my head, and in the distance, I saw Henry walking through the front doors. In my head it felt like one of those slow-motion moments that you see at the end of all the romantic comedies. He was somehow even more attractive than he was the day I left for L.A. in his gray chinos and black dress shirt. And, for once, he wasn't so pale that the sun was reflecting off his skin and into my eyes.

"Henry, it's good to see you."

"You too."

"You're looking really . . . healthy."

Kara and Adrienne suppressed a laugh.

"Thank you?"

Kara cleared her throat. "I think I'm just gonna see how things are going with Maya. Five minutes till showtime."

"And I'm just gonna go see where that kid is with my pink drink."

Kara and Adrienne walked off in different directions, leaving me alone with Henry.

Not to toot my own horn or anything, but I got a lot of attention while I was in Los Angeles, and had no problem flirting every once in a while, but for some reason I never knew what to say around Henry.

I was just one big ball of awkward.

"How was California?"

"It was nice. A lot of sun."

"Does that mean you'll be making the move a more permanent thing or —"

"You know, as much as I really liked being so close to the beach and all the sun, I also really like having all four seasons and not just grossness all year long. So, I think I might be sticking around here. At least for a little while."

"Cool." He crept around the room and slid his hands across the bookshelves, eyeing the poster of my fat head as he went.

I could've killed Maya for doing that.

"I take it since you're not going back that you're not seeing anyone from over there?"

"Well, I was seeing this actor and we said we'd try to make it work."

"Oh." His shoulders drooped a bit.

"I'm kidding. If I was seeing someone, I would've told you that. What about you?"

"Free as a bird." He turned and looked at me. "Although, there is this one guy I've had my eye on for a while."

"Really? Tell me more."

"We tried things once. Even kinda told him I was falling for him, but it wasn't really the best time for us. Now that we're both at different points in our lives, I'm thinking maybe we're in a good place to try something again."

He inched closer toward me with every word until we were face-to-face. I could feel his breath against my cheek and his fingers brushed against my hand.

"Well, I'm thinking he'd be stupid if he didn't want that. And who knows, he might have fallen for you too. He might even tell you that if he was given the chance to."

His fingers brushed the back of my head and he looked into my eyes. He scooched closer until there was only a few inches left between us.

It was my chance to finally say it. "I love you, Henry. I'm *in* love with you and I think I have been since the first moment we met. It took me going away and missing you every single day for me to realize that." My stomach churned and a knot formed in my throat. "And I'm so sorry it took me so long to realize that."

He pulled me in closer, leaving very little space between us. "You're incredibly cheesy, you know that?" His lips met mine and his hands ran through my hair. His heart beat rapidly against mine as he pulled back. "But that's one of the reasons I love you."

"You love me?"

He just nodded, pulled me in for another kiss.

"It's time," Maya said, rushing back to the front of the store. "Open the doors."

I shot him a smile and made myself comfortable in the chair, despite my stomach still doing cartwheels. The doors were unlocked, and the masses started piling in.

Henry turned back. "Hey, are you doing anything tonight?"

"I don't think so."

"What do you say about taking a picnic up to the roof?"

"Are you asking me out on a date, Henry Moore?"

"Maybe I am." He flashed a smile. "So, what do you say? Dinner at seven?"

"Seven sounds great."

I didn't know for sure if things would be like they were before, or even if Henry really was my happily ever after. Now that I think about it, there were quite a few things I didn't know. The one thing I did know though, was that for the first time in my entire life I really didn't want to have my life all mapped out.

I was excited for the surprise and I was going to enjoy the ride life was taking me on, wherever it chose to take me next.

Alex Blades is from a small, cornfield-covered town in Central Illinois. As the youngest of six kids, Alex often spent his time entertaining himself with new books, 90s reruns, and cheesy romantic comedies, so it was no surprise when he decided to try his hand at writing his own stories. When Alex isn't writing or working as a teaching assistant, he enjoys spending time with family, binge-watching his favorite shows on Netflix, and taking long, soothing strolls through the local Target.

Printed in the USA
CPSIA information can be obtained
at www.ICGtesting.com
CBHW011909140924
14363CB00014B/383